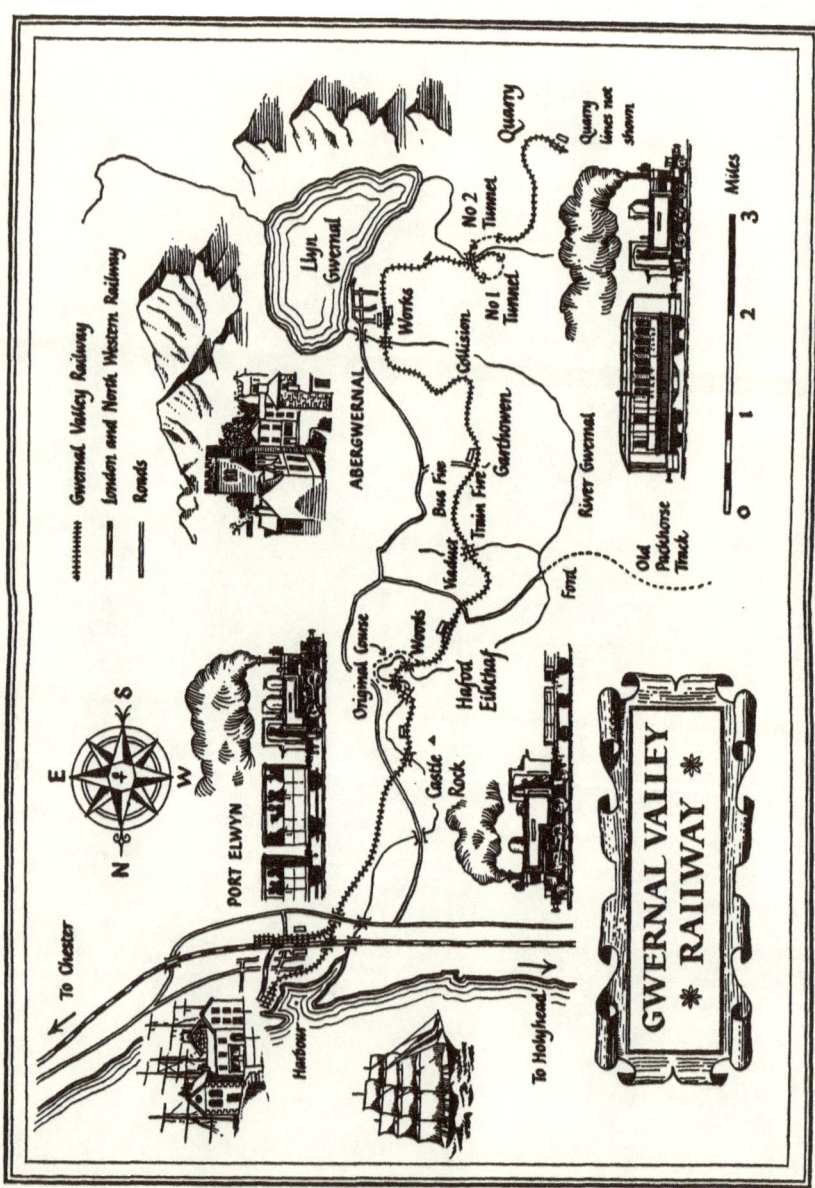

# JENNIE

## J. B. SNELL

*Illustrated by* **G. K. Sewell**

Camden Miniature Steam Services.

Other titles by J.B. Snell include:

One Man's Railway
Railway Mechanical Engineering
Britain's Railways Under steam
Early Railways
Festiniog Railway Revival (with P.B. Whitehouse)
Narrow-Gauge Railways of the British Isles (with P.B. Whitehouse)
Mixed Gauges

British Library Cataloguing-in-Publication-Data:
a catalogue record of this book is held by the British Library.

First Printing by Thomas Nelson and Sons Ltd 1958
Second Printing 2009

ISBN No. 978-0-9564073-0-6
Published in Great Britain by

CAMDEN MINIATURE STEAM SERVICES
Barrow Farm, Rode, Frome, Somerset. BA11 6PS
www.camdenmin.co.uk

Camden stock one of the widest selections of fine transportation,
engineering and other books; contact them at the above address for
a copy of their latest free Booklist.

Printed by Lightning Source, Milton Keynes

# PART ONE

## NOTE TO THE FIRST EDITION

NOBODY in this book is intended to portray any actual person, whether now alive or dead.

On the other hand, although the Gwernal Valley Railway never existed either, certain facts about it, and incidents which took place on it, have had their counterparts on various narrow-gauge railways, past or present, at home and abroad. And while there never was such a locomotive as *Jennie* on any railway, there were many people like Mr. Pearson who built some even odder ones.

Oxford, *October 1953* - Wrexham, *July 1956*                     J.B.S.

## NOTE TO THE 2009 EDITION

EVEN SO, and although much embroidered, there is no denying that indirectly the book grew out of the first three years of the Talyllyn Railway in "preservation", on which I was one of the early staff members (that is, while not being an undergraduate); indeed I was the lesser half of the crew of the only working locomotive for its first few days under the new management.

But we thought we were guarding the last few embers of a tradition, and never dreamed that fifty years later almost every other public narrow-gauge railway in Wales would have been at least partly raised from the dead, and some new ones created. So I apologise for adding yet another, which never existed. Still, to provide its surroundings along the North Wales coastline has only involved shifting a range of mountains or two (not very far), and locating another trout-filled river, plus some modifications to the local geology, all in keeping with the area's real character. I see no need to apologise for that, and we haven't changed a word.

Dymchurch, *September 2009*                     J.B.S.

## I

THERE had been many changes in the valley during the last twelve months, and in Abergwernal, the cluster of little grey-slate houses which was all that could as yet be called a village, the talk was of little else. As long as anyone could remember there had been a slate quarry in the mountains above the village, but it had been more or less common property, worked in their spare time by anybody who wanted to repair a roof. Now a company had been formed in London to take the quarry over and enlarge it. There was a big seam of blue-green slate there, they said, which was as good as any from Llanberis or Bethesda. But to become profitable, the place would have to be worked on a much bigger scale. It was no use continuing to rely on packhorses, carrying a few slabs at a time down the steep trackway to the sea. The slate would have to be made accessible, they said ; and that meant a railway.

So a small band of men armed with an Act of Parliament, and large-scale maps and plans, had worked their way up from the coast, blazing a trail with little wooden pegs driven into the ground every hundred feet. Later an army of labourers arrived and set up untidy camps in the fields—a thousand uncouth navvies, Irish and English, who outnumbered the valley folk by four to one. And when the noises of riot and revelry arose on Saturday nights children were kept indoors and shutters barred, and the locals were amazed at the wild behaviour. It was as if the heathen city of Gomorrah had been set down in their quiet land to lend conviction to the sermons in Chapel.

But the men and their camps moved up the valley in stages from Port Elwyn on the coast, and left in their wake a raw, narrow scar along the green fields and woodlands. Building a railway is a slow job now, and doubly slow in those days, when muscles, picks and shovels had to do what is done nowadays by bulldozers, grab cranes and pneumatic drills. Near the coast the land was fairly level, and there was no hard rock to cut through ; the navvies had only to dig earth out of the shallow cuttings, load it into barrows, and dump it a few chains farther along on to the low embankments. When the right of way was clear and level, and wound gently through the foothills, they moved on towards the mountains, where some real work was waiting for them. And as they moved on a smaller gang of men followed, spreading ballast and laying sleepers and rails, and when these men had finished the railway had begun.

Of course, it wasn't much of a railway yet, since even after a year's work the rails still ran only four of the seven miles to Abergwernal, and no trains had yet run. Nor, perhaps, would it ever be much of a railway in comparison with the main line along the coast, because it was in miniature : a narrow-gauge line, whose rails were only two feet apart. And the few wagons which stood about in the sidings at Port Elwyn were less than half the size of the main-line ones.

However, it was these things which interested a thin trickle of prosperous-looking men with brief-cases and top hats who came to look at the progress of the works. There were admittedly other small railways working in other parts of the country at the time, but they were still a wonder to many men. Not only to the contractors and financiers and engineers and working men who had made them their livelihood, but also to people from overseas, who knew that since a narrow-gauge line could be built more quickly and cheaply in difficult country, one might be possible where a standard-gauge line was not. So these men came to the country where the narrow-gauge railway was born, to see for themselves. And the locals, who till then had rather resented all the disturbance, grew proud of their little line and began to chatter about it to every stranger who came.

The Abergwernal quarries were not the only ones which had needed a quick and easy way of moving the slates away before they could be worked profitably. Some seventy years before this story begins, the owner of the Bethesda quarries, near Bangor in Caernarvonshire, built a two-foot-gauge tramway to the sea, and proved that this was the answer to the transport problem. Later, when locomotives proved to be better than horses, the greybeards all said that it would be impossible to run them on such a narrow gauge, and for thirty years everybody believed them, until the manager of another narrow-gauge railway, at Festiniog near by, was impudent enough to build one and prove that it worked. After this encouragement, narrow-gauge railways began to be built all over the world, and the Abergwernal line was just one of them.

In May 1876 the rails reached Abergwernal village, and the first locomotive steamed up the valley on a trial run. By the end of the month the station was completed, together with the engine shed and the building which was intended both for the company's offices and the manager's house. This had already been occupied. The General Manager had arrived on the first train of all, and the Engineer was there as well to direct construction work.

The navvies were still busy driving the railway into the mountains. This had been a very difficult part of the line to survey, and was proving an expensive and difficult one to build. There were two tunnels to drive through the rock, and several bridges and viaducts; and in one place the line, in order to gain height without distance, had to form a complete circle and cross over itself in a spiral. In the intervals he could spare from supervising work here, the Chief Engineer had to keep an eye on the building of the machine shop where the locomotives and rolling stock were to be repaired; and whenever he was deeply engaged in some tricky operation here, there was sure to be a crisis in the village, where rows of houses were being built for the quarrymen to live in.

In contrast, the General Manager seemed to be having a fairly easy time. His chief duties were apparently to keep the directors in London as happy as possible by writing them frequent reports on how smoothly work was proceeding, and to show around the gentlemen in top hats who came to inspect things, keeping them out of the way of his harassed colleague. But one morning early in June he decided that, with the opening of the railway not two months off, it was time for him to recruit some labour to run it, and with this intention he put up a large notice in the village:

## NOTICE

*The Gwernal Valley Railway Company invite applications
for employment on their railway. Applicants, who should
not be less than fifteen nor more than thirty-five years of age,
should give an account of any previous experience of railway
work they may have had, and produce references. They
should apply to the General Manager at the Company's
offices between 9 and 11 a.m. on June 10th. The rates of
remuneration will be dependent on age and qualifications.*

*By order of the directors*

WILLIAM PARKER, *Gen. Mangr.*

Perhaps it was as well that Mr Parker did not need very
many men at first, since it was not likely that anybody in
Abergwernal had had any railway experience. In fact,
some of them had never seen a train before, although the
coast line was only seven miles away.

One of the first to read the notice was a short, dark-
haired lad just turned fifteen, whose name was Owen
Roberts. He had been expecting it to go up for several
weeks, since he had already asked Mr Parker's secretary
for a job—only to be told brusquely that a notice would
be put up when men were needed, and that anyway he
looked too young. But even so, he had spent a lot of
time loitering round the railway, watching the men at
work and going as close to the engine as the driver would
let him. His father didn't like this behaviour very much,
since he missed the lad's help on the farm, but he didn't
argue, because his wife would have taken Owen's part.
For their son had always wanted to be a railwayman ; he
had seen trains on the coast line, and would have tried to
get a job there when he was old enough if the Gwernal
Valley line had not been closer to home. He was a bright
lad, and by the time he left school he had been able to

7

read, write and solve problems in arithmetic very nearly as well as the old teacher in the valley school. His parents were poor folk, making a meagre living from the lean sheep on their hill farm, and his mother realised that the job Owen had set his heart on was the key to a better life than theirs.

So, for one reason or another, there were no complaints when he deserted the farm now and then and roamed along the railway, and not even when he made friends with some of the navvies. For their wildness did not mean that they were all wicked, and a few were pleased to find one of the valley folk who was not hostile. They took him into their tents, and answered his questions; and by the beginning of June he had absorbed quite a lot of practical knowledge about railways from them—although this was interlarded with a certain amount of impractical nonsense, as they could hardly resist spinning yarns to a boy who, eager for knowledge, would believe almost anything he was told. And so Owen, even before applying for a job, was quite a well-known figure on the railway. Even Mr Parker had noticed him from time to time, but never quite had the heart to turn him off the property.

When he had finished reading the notice, Owen turned round and ran, bright-eyed, along the road towards his home. He darted up the steep path that led to the farm, which he had often tried to run up before. But it was too long and steep even after a fresh start, and after running from the village he had to slow to a walk after a moment or two. By the time he reached the door he was winded, and had to fling himself down to recover. As he did so his mother came in from the other room.

'Good heavens, Owen, what's happened?' she said. 'Has the little engine blown up, then? Or have you been told to stop loitering?'

'No, Mother—he's put up a notice—they want me to

go—to apply for—to see him on Wednesday—to get a job——'

'Ah, so that notice has been put up at last, then, has it? What do they say about references and that? Will they take you?'

Owen caught his breath and sat up. 'Yes, the notice did say something about references. What can I do about that?'

'The only person who could give you one would be Evans the School. I don't suppose they would take any notice of what your father said.'

'Old Mr Evans?' said Owen doubtfully. 'Well, I'll ask him. But I've learnt a lot about railways, anyhow, down there—which should help, surely?'

'Perhaps. But be sure and ask him for a letter to give to Mr Parker. And now go and help your father outside while I get dinner ready. There is a lot to do before tonight.'

Owen rose silently and went off as he was told; after all, it wouldn't be long now before he was free of farm work. His mother turned back to the kitchen; but she was not thinking about how difficult it would be on the farm without Owen's help. His sister could still lend a hand. The urgent question now was, what should he wear for the interview? The only possible answer was the suit which his father had worn for their wedding and only once since; and it would need a lot of tailoring to fit Owen. Anyhow, surely Mr Parker would understand that nobody in this valley could afford to dress as smartly as city folk.

So on Wednesday morning Owen, unnaturally well washed and brushed, was walking self-consciously down the village street, trying to take no notice of a tail of school-children who were trailing him and mocking his old-fashioned suit. The devil take women who dressed you up in stupid clothes, he was thinking. All his self-confidence seemed to have been washed out of him as well; what if Mr Parker, who had seen him in his ordinary clothes, should hoot with laughter when he saw him in this rig and send him away? What if he should say the wrong thing? What if all the jobs had already been taken?

By the time he reached the office he was certain that he was merely wasting his time, and that he might as well go straight back to the farm and stay there. He hardly dared knock on the door, and nearly ran away when the clerk opened it; but after a moment he found himself standing in a small, empty room, giving his name and address. For the clerk was a kindly man, and saw what the trouble was.

'Sit down and make yourself comfortable here,' he said. 'Mr Parker will see you in a minute. You're the first this morning. And,' he added in a lower voice, 'don't be frightened of him—he might bark a little but he can't bite you, and he's always in a good mood after breakfast.'

Owen summoned up a faint smile and sat down to wait.

The actual interview, ten minutes later, was not nearly so bad as he had feared. Mr Parker was a man of about forty, and had a thick bushy beard which made him look much fiercer than in fact he was.

'*Hrrm!* You! Yes. Seen you before, haven't I? Been loitering round the railway for weeks, hey? Still, never had any complaints. Sit down there. Do your parents live here?'

'Yes, sir: at Penrhiw, on that hill above the station.'

'Ah, yes. Go to school here?'

'Yes, sir.'

'How old were you when you left school?'

'Twelve, sir, but getting on for thirteen.'

'Can you read and write?'

'Why, yes, sir,' answered Owen with some surprise.

'Very well, read this—first column, page seven,' Mr Parker said, handing over a copy of *The Times*. Owen had never seen a daily paper before, but read out a paragraph (about the Fleet being sent to terrify the Turks) without much trouble except for a bad stumble over 'Constantinople'.

'All right, that's enough,' said Mr Parker. 'Now take this pen and start copying out the next paragraph.'

Owen did this for a minute or two, his tongue following the letters as he made them. He had written five lines and made only one blot when Mr Parker said, 'That's enough—now show it to me.'

'It 'll do,' he added after a glance. 'Now. Why do you want to work for us?'

This was rather an unanswerable question, and Owen could only mumble that he had always wanted to work on a railway.

'*Hmmm*. Well, "always" is a long time, boy, but I see what you mean. What job do you want to do on the railway, then?'

Owen's heart quickened slightly as he answered, 'I'd like to work on the engines, sir.'

'Ha, naturally. You lads always do. Still, there is a vacancy, and I'll give you a trial. Can you start to-morrow?'

'Yes, sir!' said Owen, a triumphant smile on his face.

'Right, then. Get yourself a pair of overalls and heavy boots, and a cap, and be at the engine shed at half past six tomorrow morning. At first you will be a cleaner, and if you do well you will be paid one and twopence a day. If you do well enough to be promoted, we may see about increasing this later. Have you any questions?'

'No, sir. Thank you very much indeed, sir!'

'Don't thank me, my lad—just try and give satisfaction.

That's all, now. On your way out, ask Mr Simmons to give you a rule book, and read it through tonight.'

And with that the interview was over. When he had been given his little blue rule book Owen dashed off and, regardless of his fine clothes, ran home, this time without slowing to a walk. His demand for working-clothes caused some disturbance. The bottom of the family money-box had to be scraped to buy a pair of overalls; and so it was just as well that he already possessed a cap and a serviceable pair of boots.

## II

Owen was hardly able to sleep that night; he got up at first light and arrived at the engine shed at six instead of half past. There was nobody astir, and the door was locked, so he sat down outside to wait. After a quarter of an hour a burly red-headed man appeared through the gate and walked towards him, swinging a bunch of keys. Owen recognised him as the driver, since he had seen him often enough before on the engine, when they were bringing up loads of building materials, or rails and sleepers. He was a Scot, named Angus Duncan, who had been sent to Abergwernal by the firm who built the locomotive.

'Good morning, sir,' Owen said diffidently.

'And good morning to you,' said the red-headed man, catching sight of him. 'Don't "sir" me, either. Are you Owen Roberts?'

'Yes, I am.'

'I've been told about you. Follow me.'

Owen followed him through the door, and walked behind him towards the locomotive, which stood cold and silent at the far end of the shed. He had seen her before, but not so closely as this. He followed Duncan, gazing at her curiously. But he didn't have time to notice very much, because Duncan waved his arm in the direction of a large pile of firewood stacked against the wall.

'Get a couple of armloads of that and put them on the footplate in the cab,' he said, and walked off. When Owen had done this he returned, carrying a small shovel filled with bits of greasy rag. He set this down beside the wood.

'I'm now going to light the engine up, as we say—so watch what I do. For if you want to stay here you will have to learn to do this job yourself,' he said. Owen said nothing, so he continued: 'The first thing you must always do before setting a fire in the engine is to make sure there's water in the boiler, because if you light a fire in an empty boiler you burn it, and that would be the end of you. You see here the gauge glass—you see the water in it? Well, that looks all right, but you've got to make sure, so you open this cock, so, and drain it.' Owen watched and heard a trickling of water somewhere beneath him as Duncan opened the valve. After a moment he shut it again; the trickling stopped and water suddenly rose into the glass again.

'Well, that's all right,' Duncan was saying. 'I've drained the glass, and it's filled again, so we can be sure that there's water in the boiler.'

With that he struck a match and lit the rags. As soon as the flames had caught he tossed them into the firebox, and threw wood in on top of them. A cloud of pungent grey smoke rolled out and set Owen's eyes watering. He backed out of the cab, blinking. After piling on the wood Duncan threw in a dozen or so lumps of coal and slammed the firedoor shut. As he did so a cloud of thick smoke began to ooze slowly out of the chimney. Some of it found its way out through louvres in the roof, but most started to form a choking fog in the shed. Owen started to cough.

'Never mind, lad, you'll get used to it,' said Duncan. 'There's no more to be done for a wee while now, so I had better show you around the engine. First of all, she was built in Glasgow, as you'll see.'

Owen had seen already; a shining brass plate on the side of the cab said: CHARLES PEARSON & CO : UNION WORKS : GLASGOW, 1876. Immediately above, another brass plate told the locomotive's name, which, as he had long known, was *Lady Margaret*.

Then Duncan conducted him on a circular tour of the locomotive, and explained in detail what each part did, and how it worked. Owen had picked up a smattering of knowledge about this from a book he had seen once; but with no more than a smattering he was as much confused as helped by the flow of words at first. But after a while, as he saw everything in front of him, some of his old jumble of ideas slipped into place. Duncan showed him the valve gear and springing, which involved a descent into the pit beneath the engine and peering into awkward corners lit only by a smoky flare. He showed him the arrangements in the smokebox, and in a few suffocating moments Owen saw how the exhaust steam was directed up the chimney so as to increase the draught in the firebox. Then finally Duncan led him into the cab and lectured him on what was to be found there. Owen avoided asking silly questions mainly by luck, but after half an hour was beginning to piece things together, so that Duncan began to be satisfied with his progress.

'Well, we'll make a fireman of you yet,' he said eventually.

'I hope so, Mr Duncan,' said Owen.

'Good—but don't call me Mr Duncan : call me Angus, and leave the mistering to the Manager.' He paused for a moment, and then went on, 'This one's quite a good engine, with all the new gadgets. Look at this wee thing here, which you'll have to learn to work later, when she's got steam. It's an injector, and it feeds water into the boiler, like the axle pump I showed you—but this one uses a jet of steam, which just blows the water in. You can only use the pump when the engine is moving, but you can use the injector when she's standing still as well.'

Then they left *Lady Margaret* to herself for a while, and Angus showed Owen around the buildings. In the main shed, where they were, there were two tracks and room for four engines, each standing over a pit about five feet deep and six feet wide, where the rails were carried by girders. Here it was easy to get underneath the engines to do any minor repairs, oiling, and so on. Around the walls were barrels of oil, sacks of cotton waste, firewood, and a great number of other stores for which Owen could imagine no use at all. Everything was still fresh and clean, but each day the swirling smoke and steam laid another thin coat of grime over walls and floor. In an adjoining shed was a lot of machinery : lathes, drills, shaping machines, a forge with an enormous pair of bellows to blow it, and a quantity of other equipment, some still being installed.

16

The men were at work in here, and it looked as if they had enough to do to keep them busy for some weeks yet.

At eight o'clock Angus consulted his large turnip watch and set Owen to work polishing the brass and cleaning the paint on *Lady Margaret*, which was clean by modern standards before he started and remarkably so after he had done. Angus busied himself with oiling up, and clambered around and underneath clutching two canisters of oil and grease, whistling the first two lines of 'The Campbells are coming' again and again, very slowly through his teeth. It was not very pleasant to listen to. At half past eight the boiler started making rumbling noises; Angus consulted his watch again and said, 'Nearly two hours from cold—a bit slow this morning,' then climbed into the cab and turned on the blower. Owen was polishing the brass band round the back of the smokebox, and was taken by surprise when a sooty shower of lukewarm water gurgled out of the chimney.

*Lady Margaret* was now beginning to show signs of life. The blower was working, its hiss growing louder each minute as steam pressure built up. Owen could see a bright red glare coming through the open dampers as the fire blazed up with the draught and sat back contentedly until he should be told what to do next. After a moment Angus, having finished oiling, joined him.

'What we have to do today is this. Yesterday the other two locomotives arrived at Port Elwyn, and we've got to go and fetch them up here. We'll have to haul them dead, as they must be checked over before we can use them. Four coaches have come, too, and since Mr Parker wants everything brought up today we'll have quite a load.'

'What are the other two engines like?' asked Owen.

'Well, I've never seen them, mind you, but I used to be with the Union works, where they were built, and when

17

I came here with this one they were talking of building another like her. I suppose she'll be the same in most ways : six driving wheels with a carrying wheel at each end, and weigh the same twenty ton. But what the third one 'll be like I can't say. Mr Pearson was keeping quiet, but they said he had some bee in his bonnet about her.'

With that Angus climbed into the cab. Owen followed him, and saw that the pressure gauge read 35 lb. out of a maximum of 120.

'She should shift now,' said Angus, 'but before you move an engine that's been standing still for any time you must open the cylinder cocks, so that the water can get out easily.' He checked the position of the rod at the side of the cab which worked them, and then pulled the reversing lever back and opened the regulator gently. Slowly, with a rushing of steam and water from the open cocks, *Lady Margaret* moved out of the shed and stopped beside the water tank. Owen had climbed into the cab so as not to miss his first ride on a locomotive, even if it was a journey of only fifty feet. Now he was set to the not very exciting task of refilling the bunker with coal from a truck which stood on the next siding, while Angus, after checking the level of water in the tanks, stood by and lit a pipe.

A few minutes later Mr Parker and the Chief Engineer, whose name was Sullivan, appeared. 'Good morning, Duncan,' said the first. 'No need to take much down with us today ; just the van. We'll travel in that. Couple on to it, and I'll be back in a few minutes.'

Unlike his companion, Mr Sullivan was wearing overalls, and looked as if he was prepared to do some work. He was an older man, in his middle forties, and a Londoner. He belonged to a firm of consulting engineers who had been called in to superintend the construction and fitting-out of the railway, and while work was in progress he had been sent down to take charge of it.

18

'No troubles to report this morning, Mr Duncan, I hope?' he said.

'No, sir—she's been a real lady so far.'

'Good. Now, on the way down I want you to stop at the viaduct just this side of Hafod Eithaf. The contractor says he's been having trouble with it, and I want to see it for myself.'

'Very well, sir.'

'Right, then.' Mr Sullivan turned away and went into the shed. Angus drew noisily on his pipe for a moment, then called to Owen.

'Haven't you finished coaling her yet, lad?'

'I don't think I can get much more on now,' Owen answered.

'Then come over here and I'll show you how to work the injectors.'

Owen climbed down and watched. Angus opened a valve, and a round tube of water fell smoothly out of the waste pipe. He let it fall for a moment, then flicked another valve rapidly open. There was a click, the water stopped flowing, and after a moment a shrill singing noise began.

'Got him!' Angus said. 'They're wonderful inventions, but often tricky to start. And sometimes they won't start at all and you have to use the pump. Now, we've got enough water, very nearly, so I'll turn it off and you try to see if you can start it again.'

He did so, and Owen took his place. But he found it wasn't as easy as it looked. Twice he failed to open the steam valve quickly enough, and an angry jet of steam whinnied out of the overflow. The third time he tried again and it worked. Angus grunted, told him to turn it off, and then delivered another short lecture:

'Now, you must always keep your eye on the level of the water, and never let it get out of sight in the gauge glass. For if it goes over the top the engine will prime, and blow water out of the chimney and damage the valves; and if it gets too low, the firebox will burn and you'll blow yourself up. That's the most important of the three things you will have to remember. The second is to keep the fire hot, and keep the steam pressure high, which comes with practice, and the third is not to let her blow away too much steam at the safety valves. If you do, you'll waste coal and water and make your own work harder as well. Now, have you understood everything I've told you?'

'I think so.'

'Well, I don't suppose you have, but you'd better do so soon.'

With that Angus blew a hoot on the whistle, and they moved off. Owen jumped down to change the points. These were not yet controlled from the signal box, which was still being built, and he had to lean against a small hand lever which had been connected to them for the time being. Angus started to shout at him not to let the lever go while the locomotive was on the points, but he saw that the warning wasn't needed. Owen was pushing with enthusiasm; in fact, while he had been loitering round the railway during the previous months he had seen two navvies, pushing a trolley loaded with rails, come to grief through running it over split points, and he had learnt that lesson the easy way. He had also enlarged his vocabulary, since they had started quarrelling over whose fault it was, and when they had finished calling each other names they repeated them at the trolley, while they laboriously unloaded it, rerailed it, and loaded it up again.

*Lady Margaret* backed down gently on to the van, and Owen coupled it on. Again, he had seen this done before, and so knew more or less how to do it. He found it was simple enough: slipping the link on the locomotive into the hook on the van, and tightening up on the screw until the buffers touched. Angus watched him critically, and when he had finished he tested the tightness of the coupling with his foot.

They climbed back into the cab, and backed slowly down the line towards the unfinished platform, stopping before they reached it. By now work had started for the day, and many men were about. Two old men were at work on the slate edging for the platform, chipping away at large slabs to make them fit into each other. Another man was painting the wooden building, covering the ugly pink undercoating with a dark brown. Looking up the line towards the quarries, Owen saw the gang of platelayers at work ; beyond them ran a bare grey path, curving out of sight—the completed roadbed. Angus blew three long blasts on the whistle, as a sign that they were ready and waiting ; in the silence which followed Owen could hear the angry cawing of rooks in the wood on the hillside, alarmed by the unusual noise. He turned and looked at the fire, putting a few shovelfuls of coal just inside the door, as he had been told. Trying to look as if he had done it all his life, he consulted the water and pressure gauges, and sat back comfortably.

After a few minutes Mr Parker and Mr Sullivan re-appeared and climbed into the van. Mr Sullivan dumped a large toolbox he was carrying on the floor, and leant out of the window on Owen's side. ' Right away ! ' he said. ' And tell Mr Duncan not to forget to stop at the viaduct.'

With a light load *Lady Margaret* accelerated quickly, and rattled over the points at the end of the yard at a fair speed. The track had only just been laid and had not yet settled, so they rocked and rolled a bit and Angus did not go very fast. Owen leant out of the swaying cab and felt that the millenium had come. He had lived for this moment for months, and imagined often what it would be like. Now it was the real thing : here he was at last, riding on a bouncing locomotive and rocketing down the narrow track. The sun shone and the breeze ran through his hair ; he had never felt better pleased with life. He looked back, and saw the grey haze coming out of the chimney turn into a plume of white steam ; and underneath, the little grey van rolled sullenly behind them while, beyond it in turn, the track shrank into the distance. Then he looked forward again, as they leant over to take a curve, and ducked his head in as they shot under a bridge. This provided another excuse for consulting the gauges ; as he did so the safety valves began to sizzle, so he turned on the feed pump. ' Good lad,' Angus said. ' I was just about to tell you to do that.'

From Abergwernal to Port Elwyn was almost exactly seven miles. The line followed the valley all the way, and was usually not too far from the river. But on leaving Abergwernal it had to climb over a ridge, where aeons ago a vast landslide had blocked the valley. This had formed the lake to the south of the village ; more than a mile long, it was now famed as one of the best trout lakes in Wales. The river had slowly cut a ravine through the ridge, and the surveyors of the railway had tried to find a route for the line through it, in order to preserve an easy gradient. But there had been no room for both railway and river, and so they had to go over the top. As a result, for a mile and a half between Abergwernal and Garthowen, the cluster of houses at the summit, where a small station had been built, the railway climbed quite steeply : at 1 in 80. Beyond, it fell even more steeply, at 1 in 60, for three miles, past Hafod Eithaf, where there was a village as large as Abergwernal had been before the railway came, and which had another station, to Castle Rock. Here there were no houses but only a crag with, on its summit, the ruins of a tower which had commanded the entrance to the valley in the olden days. For these three miles it twisted and turned to take advantage of every inequality of the ground ; for the last two and a half miles into Port Elwyn the land was nearly level, and the railway very nearly straight.

Owen still leant out of the cab, watching and trying to memorise every turn in the line. He knew the country well, of course, for he had lived in the district all his life ; but the railway took such a strange, winding route that from time to time he lost his bearings. He had walked over the track before, but he got a very different idea of it from a locomotive travelling at speed, and he was surprised to see the landmarks go flashing by so quickly. After a few more minutes the gradient eased ; they passed through a long cutting in the rock, through the little station at Garthowen, with a blast on the whistle in case anything should be moving on the by-road towards the level crossing. Then Owen was startled to see that the rails seemed to come to an end on a ledge. He held his breath for a moment, but as they drew closer he saw that in fact they began to slope steeply downward. As they rolled over the crest Angus closed the regulator and began to wind down the handbrake. Their speed continued unabated, but instead of the gentle purring of the exhaust nothing could be heard now but the roar of the wheels on the rails, the clicking of the rail joints, and the gentle rubbing of the brakes. The track started to curve, and Owen held on tightly as the locomotive swayed and lurched, nosing from one side to the other. After a couple of minutes they began to slow down. As they emerged from a cutting Angus gave the brake handle another turn, and with a final squeal from the brakes they stopped, just short of a stone viaduct of three spans over the gully of a small stream. As they drew up three of the contractor's men looked round. Mr Sullivan climbed out and went to speak with them for a few minutes; he seemed satisfied, returned to the van, and waved Angus on again.

'Next stop Port Elwyn,' said Angus, releasing the brakes. They crossed the viaduct, slowly gathered speed again on the gradient, swept past the half-finished station and sidings at Hafod Eithaf, and ran through a large wood. In the van Mr Parker and Mr Sullivan resumed their conversation.

'Well, they seem to have that particular trouble under control,' said the latter, referring to the men at the viaduct. 'The foreman thought he saw signs of the foundation on the second pier settling, but it's nothing abnormal, and they're just tidying up now. Anyhow, as I was saying, I don't much like the idea of Pearson using us as a testing ground for his new gadgets. One of the two locos we're picking up today is going to be all right, I know; it's an exact copy of this one, and from a month's acquaintance with this machine I have a very high opinion of what Pearson can do when he sticks to conventional design. But the third—I don't know. For one thing, she's too small— only four driving wheels against six, and she weighs only fifteen tons against twenty. So on these gradients she's not going to pull so much of a load.'

'That could be an advantage, you know,' Mr Parker pointed out. 'I don't suppose all our trains will be heavy —the passenger trains should be pretty light, even if we do put the ordinary goods traffic on the back. And if she works on the passenger trains she'll never have to go up the worst gradients, up beyond the village.'

'Yes, I know that, and you may be right. But her size isn't what I'm really worried about. It's his incredible three-cylinder arrangement. I'm sure I don't know what he hoped to gain by it, except I suppose it could make for free running. You see, what he's done is this: he's put three cylinders on her—the third is inside, underneath the smokebox.'

24

'What's the idea of that? Surely an ordinary engine works perfectly well with two?'

'I think what he has in mind is to offset the lightness of the engine by giving a smoother production of power —six impulses to every revolution of the wheels instead of four.'

'I see,' said Mr Parker, who scarcely understood.

'But the valve gear is extraordinary, too,' Mr Sullivan continued. 'The old man's invented some immensely complicated system of slides and levers and cranks and the Lord alone knows what, in order to get the best—or what he thinks ought to be the best—out of his idea. And that, with the untrained fitters we will have here, is not going to be easy to keep in order. Still, I'm looking forward to seeing this locomotive, though I've only seen drawings so far, and she should be interesting. But even if she does turn out to be a white elephant and we have to call her "Pearson's Folly", you'll have a great deal of entertainment keeping her on the road.' Mr Sullivan said this as if he didn't really mean it.

'Well, I hope all goes well, because you're going to show her off in front of a lot of important people next month. Pearson himself is coming down to show you how to do your job. He's written an article about his engine in this month's *Engineering*, as well.'

Mr Sullivan groaned. 'Still, if we can't get the thing to go before his state visit,' he said, 'we can always shunt it into the lake and let him play with one of his others instead.'

'That might be quite a good idea,' said Mr Parker.

There was silence for a moment, and then the conversation turned to other matters. Meanwhile the train had run out of the woods, and was rattling across the marshy fields towards the coast. Owen had made up the fire under instructions, and now leant out again watching the mountains slowly glide past on either side, and the grey roofs of the town rise out of the fields ahead of them. After a few more minutes the line skirted round the north of the town, threw off a branch which went down to the quay, and then ran up alongside the standard-gauge tracks. A main-line engine, which looked enormous in comparison with *Lady Margaret*, was standing near by. Its driver caught sight of them and watched them with amusement. As they rattled past, practically under his nose, Angus blew a blast of greeting on the whistle. Owen laughed to see the astonishment on the face of the main-line driver, aghast at such impertinence ; but nevertheless he whistled in return. They slowed down to run through the passenger station, which shared a platform with the main line, and stopped in the exchange yard just beyond. Owen caught sight of a line of coaches placed on a narrow-gauge siding ; splendid long ones they were, bright red, with end plat-forms and clerestory roofs. He dimly remembered seeing a drawing of an American train, of which they reminded him. But the coaches were not his main attention.

They stopped alongside the two new locomotives. The first was called *Lady Gwyneth*, and was the same as *Lady Margaret* ; the second was called *Jennie*, and was very different. Angus gazed at her, muttering something in Gaelic ; Owen peered over his shoulder and just gaped, for she was quite unlike any locomotive he had ever seen before.

She wouldn't have excited very much comment eighty years later, of course, when people had grown used to seeing locomotives festooned with pipes and rods and levers ; but in an age which kept everything decently from sight, and (to put the other side of the coin) indecently inaccessible, she was a shocking sight. The cab bore a family resem-blance to those on the other two locomotives ; all were good big cabs for their day, giving plenty of protection

26

from the weather. The chimney bore a family resemblance, too, except that it was crowned with a large polished copper cap, which glinted in the sunlight. The water tanks, again like the others, were ordinary side tanks, but they had been cut short at the front end in order to give access to the inside cylinder. As Mr Sullivan had said, she was a smaller machine, about three-quarters the length of her companions, and with only four driving wheels. But it was not easy to see this at first, since the wheels were obscured by one of the most strangely complicated sets of valve gear that had ever been designed, much less built.

The two men stepped out of the van and gazed at her.

' Pearson's Patent ! ' exclaimed Mr Sullivan with feeling. ' What a wonderful twisted mind the man must have ! '

Mr Parker smiled. ' I think you may want a couple of watchmakers to help you with that valve gear,' he said. 'And what are all those domes for ? '

' Sand, I expect. Well, she'll probably need it—if she ever goes at all,' was the reply. ' However, it's no good giving way to despair, I suppose ; worse things happened to Noah. Let's go and have a look.'

The two walked over and climbed up into *Jennie*'s cab. As they disappeared, Owen turned to Angus.

' What do you think of her, Mr Duncan ? ' he asked cautiously.

' I've never seen sic' an ugly brute in all my life,' was the answer. ' But that's neither here nor there. The problem is, will she do the work ? And,' he added reflectively, ' what's going to happen when some poor lost soul has to take that valve gear down ? But I'll say no more till I've driven her.'

Owen didn't answer. As a matter of fact, he thought, I rather like the look of her ; but I'd better not say so, because I've always been told not to contradict my elders.

He looked once more at the water gauge, saw that the fire had burnt low, and was starting to put some more coal on when Angus stopped him.

'No, lad, don't put any more on; we'll be standing here for a bit, and she'll do as she is. You don't want to have her blowing off and wasting steam. Stay here.' With that he picked up the two cans of oil and walked over to *Jennie*.

'What do you want me to do, sir?' he asked.

'Well, we want to take all this stuff up today if we can,' replied Mr Sullivan. 'Besides these two locomotives, there are four coaches and three transporter wagons, and we want to take all those up to try them out.'

'Transporter wagons?' asked Angus.

'Yes; the idea is that any goods traffic we have to take up the line—coal and so on—should be taken up in a standard-gauge wagon carried on one of these, to save transferring the load. It's quite a good idea, I think.'

Mr Parker said, 'I've often wondered who thought of it. Do you know?'

'No, but it's been done before,' answered Mr Sullivan. 'The Great Western had a few running on the broad gauge between Bristol and Gloucester, but this is the first time it's been done on as small a scale as this. Well,' he continued, turning back to Angus, 'do you think she'll be able to pull that load?'

'There's nothing to stop us trying.'

'Good. I think she may, myself; you've got a good dry rail, anyhow. But first of all we shall have to oil everything. Will you see to *Lady Gwyneth*, and I'll take a look at this thing.'

The two of them set to work, and Mr Parker strolled away towards the station, where he had business to transact. He met the stationmaster scurrying down the platform towards him. He was a pompous, fat little man, seriously out of breath, and conscious that he was not at his most dignified.

'Good morning, Mr Parker, sir, good morning!' he said, stretching out his hand. 'I'm sorry I wasn't here to meet you, but time-keeping on your line's shocking, shocking, not even a timetable to keep to, and I wasn't expecting you!' He wagged his head archly, and then wondered if his joke (such as it was) hadn't perhaps gone a bit too far. The Gwernal Valley company had entered the station as tenants, not in their own right, and so he and his staff were responsible for both lines. He had sourly reflected that the result was that he now had two carpets on which he could be called to stand: one at Crewe, and the other, he supposed, at Abergwernal. So he was anxious not to create a bad impression. But he was reassured.

'That's all right,' Mr Parker said good-humouredly. 'I know our feckless behaviour must make things difficult for you, but we should be settling down shortly.'

The stationmaster began to chatter again, but was suddenly cut short by a loud bellow coming from behind him.

'Hi!' shouted the voice. 'Duncan, come and get me out of this confounded booby-trap!'

'Hullo!' and 'Dear me!' said Mr Parker and the stationmaster in unison. 'That's Mr Sullivan's voice!' They hurried back to *Jennie*, just in time to see Angus grab hold of a pair of flailing legs and heave on them. Owen smothered a roar of laughter as Mr Sullivan reappeared, greasy and dishevelled.

'What an abomination!' that exasperated man said, leaving an oily black mark as he wiped his forehead. 'You mind that doesn't happen to you, Duncan. I just leaned in to oil the inside valve gear—went in perfectly easily— then found I couldn't get out! Stuck tight!' He returned to his task more warily, rubbing his bruised shoulders.

'When I finish here I'm going to go to work on the broad gauge. None of this nonsense at Swindon,' he said.

'Yes, it seems as if we really do need narrow-gauge men for narrow-gauge railways,' said Mr Parker, turning to walk away again; and the stationmaster laughed dutifully in his turn.

Angus returned to *Lady Gwyneth* with an imperfectly suppressed grin, and Owen leaned out of *Lady Margaret*'s cab and watched closely. It was ridiculous, he knew it, but somehow looking at *Jennie* he seemed to get the impression that she was amused by the incident as well. He pondered on this for a while. One of the reasons why he was fascinated by locomotives was because they seemed human, somehow; but were they as human as all that? I must be going daft, he thought.

But perhaps not, again. Some of the stories the Irishmen had told him, about engines which seemed to take a dislike to certain men, and wouldn't run well under them, appeared to bear this idea out. There was even one rather horrible story about an old locomotive that silently started moving one night with nobody near, and ran down a driver who had treated her roughly the day before. Owen wasn't so sure. . . .

Mr Sullivan finished his work without any more misadventures. It took him some time, because the job had to be done thoroughly, and he had no desire to be trapped again. The locomotives had, of course, been tested at the works (indeed Mr Pearson had laid several hundred yards of narrow-gauge track for that very purpose), and so they were in full running order. But the job took him a long time, because as he came to each strange piece of machinery he stopped to look at it. Before he had finished Angus came over, and started a similar fact-finding investigation.

'I will say this much for Pearson—his workmanship is good, and everything looks beautifully made,' said Mr

Sullivan. 'But I think that as far as this thing goes it all seems needlessly complicated. I've been trying to make out this valve arrangement—I think I see now what he wants to do. You can see for yourself. There are two slide valves for every cylinder and, what's more, there's what amounts to a separate set of gear for each valve. One obviously admits steam to the cylinder, and that's straightforward enough. But the other one is the exhaust valve, and that's not so simple at all. As far as I can see, the effect of it is to have the exhaust port fully open for practically the whole length of the return stroke, whatever the other valve is doing.'

'He's a clever man,' said Angus.

'Too clever by half, perhaps. This is ingenious, all credit for that—but I still wonder what it will be like keeping it in running order. However that may be, though, I'm beginning to think that we might be able to get some speed out of this machine—it ought to run freely enough. I'll see if we can't steam her up and take her out tomorrow or the day after, and see how she goes. Have you finished on the other one? Right—let's go and do those coaches as well.'

With that they carried their oilcans down towards the coaches. These had been built by Pearson also, for he had contracted to supply all the rolling stock for the line. The coaches, as Owen had guessed, were the result of a visit to America a few years before. They were long, bogie vehicles, and unlike those which ran on the Festiniog Railway, it was possible for a tall man to stand upright in them. They were entered from verandahs at each end, and a corridor ran down the middle. The fourth was different from the others : one end was converted into a compartment for luggage and the guard, and the other end was labelled FIRST CLASS. Angus looked in through the window, and saw that the seats in here were upholstered, and in one

31

corner he saw too a pot-bellied stove, with a chimney poking through the roof.

'Should get plenty of first class in winter, anyhow,' said Mr Parker, noticing it as well. 'Sullivan, the stationmaster tells me that they have another four wagonloads of sleepers and a load of rails ready for us. That makes ten of our wagons full of sleepers, as well as three of those bogie flats with the rails. And he says he's expecting some more tomorrow, so he'd like these out of the way. Can we manage to take them up with us today?'

'Ask the driver,' answered Mr Sullivan. 'But if we have to, we can do it, even if it means taking the train up the hill in two halves.'

'It's all right with me,' said Angus. 'Truth to tell, I'd rather like to see how much she will pull; we've never had a really heavy load on before.'

'You'll have one today, and no mistake,' said Mr Sullivan. 'Two locomotives to start with : that makes thirty-five tons—one at twenty and the other at fifteen. Four coaches at seven apiece : twenty-eight—sixty-three. Ten loads of sleepers, thirty—ninety-three. Three of rails, say twenty-three—a hundred and sixteen. And then three transporters. They'll be about three and a half each, say ten—so with the van that makes about a hundred and twenty-eight tons. The train will weigh more than six times as much as the engine.'

'Tally-ho!' said Mr Parker.

'It should be possible,' said Angus. 'It's been done before, but not so often on three miles of one-in-sixty. We can but try.'

An hour later Mr Sullivan was satisfied with the running condition of all the new rolling stock.

'Duncan, Mr Parker and I are going off for lunch now,' he said. 'We'll be back about one o'clock, I expect. Will you have the train marshalled by then? Have the locomotives first, then the coaches, and then the transporters and the track materials.'

' Right, sir—it shall be ready.'

While they disappeared in the direction of Port Elwyn's one and only eating-house, Angus returned to *Lady Margaret*, where Owen was still waiting patiently for something to happen.

' Well, lad, have you brought your dinner with you ? '

Owen answered that he had, but that he had eaten it long ago ; sometime about the middle of the afternoon, he thought.

' Away with you—it's not twelve yet. I'm having mine now. If you like, leave the engine to me and go and have a look round the yard. But don't be longer than twenty minutes, because we have some shunting to do.'

Owen gratefully disappeared, and began an exploration on his own account. He went on to the standard-gauge station, and watched an express, hauled by an Allan single-wheeler, roar through at fifty miles an hour, sparks flying from the chimney, and a pall of dust and black smoke in its wake.

Good heavens ! he thought : I've never seen one go as fast as that before, nor will I, working on a narrow-gauge line. It's a bit much to ask fifty miles an hour from our engines. Look at their driving wheels, only two-foot-six as against seven feet. But still, speed isn't everything.

Then he returned to the Gwernal Valley side of the station, and inspected the two new locomotives. His liking for *Jennie* was increased the more he looked at her ; she seemed more compact, better proportioned, somehow, underneath all the plumbing. But he hadn't much time, and for the last five minutes he looked at the coaches and wagons, and noted the layout of the sidings. He hadn't been down to the coast since they had started building the little railway, and things had changed a great deal. Twenty minutes must be up by now ; he ran back towards *Lady Margaret*.

Angus was brushing some breadcrumbs out of his beard. ' You let the fire go very low while you were waiting,' he said. ' Stoke it up now, and it will burn through by the time we start.'

Owen did as he was told. He also used the injector to fill up the boiler ; this time he got it going at the first attempt. By the time the gauge glass was full the pressure had dropped to sixty pounds. Owen asked whether this mattered, or whether he should turn on the blower a little harder.

' Eh ? Oh, no, leave her be—time enough for the blower later. Do you know what they call it where I come from ? They call it the Fireman's Friend, since he can use it to cover up his mistakes. But she'll do as she is for shunting.'

They then set about marshalling the train, which proved a long job, as they had some complicated shunting to do. Angus drove, and Owen held over the point levers and made the couplings. Eventually they had the complete train assembled in the correct order, with the two dead locomotives leading, and were just putting the little grey van on the other end when Mr Parker and Mr Sullivan returned. Mr Parker came up and told Angus not to go faster than ten miles an hour, and to keep a constant watch on the train in case anything should go wrong. Owen had to resort to using the Fireman's Friend to get the pressure up in time, but now they had a good fire and were ready to go.

Mr Sullivan, who seemed to be a very long way off at the far end of the train, got into the van and waved his hand, and Angus opened the regulator. *Lady Margaret* started slowly until the slack had been taken out of the couplings; then Angus opened up a little more and they began to accelerate. She slipped once; then she gripped the rails firmly, and with a determined roaring from the chimney they were under way once more. Angus pulled back the reversing lever, gave the 'thumbs up' sign to Owen, and said, 'You'd better keep an eye on the fire this time, my lad—we shall be burning a lot more coal this trip.' Owen nodded. 'And I don't want to have to divide the train.'

The first level two and a half miles passed fairly easily. *Lady Margaret* was pulling strongly, and Angus was pleased to see that the pressure never dropped below a hundred and fifteen pounds. The long train trailed smoothly behind them. Men working in the fields turned to stare at the strange sight as it rolled past; then suddenly they were in the hills. *Lady Margaret* lifted her nose to the grade; *Lady Gwyneth* and *Jennie* followed her, and one by one the coaches and wagons tilted upwards and hung on her drawbar; passive, dead weight. Angus opened the regulator as wide as it would go, and then dropped the reversing lever forward notch by notch until after a couple of minutes it also could go no farther. 'It's up to her ladyship now,' he said; 'she's got the lot.'

*Lady Margaret* bellowed and barked, and shot a column of steam and black smoke straight into the air, rattling the branches of trees overhanging the line. The speed fell slowly, but finally remained steady at about five miles an hour. Angus looked anxiously at the pressure gauge, but was relieved to see that it was not dropping. Owen had the feed pump working continuously, but in spite of that the level of the water in the glass dropped imperceptibly. If he had been on a standard-gauge engine being worked as hard, Owen realised that he would be shovelling coal into the firebox for all he was worth, and that even so it would be burnt, or thrown out of the chimney, faster than

35

he could bale it in. But on *Lady Margaret* the situation was not nearly so desperate ; every two minutes or so he would put on five shovelfuls of coal, as Angus had shown him ; two under the door, one at the front, and one at each side, and would then slam the door shut and rest. Even so, he needed to cool down ; the fire was a violent blazing white, and having the door open even for a few seconds made the heat in the cab almost insufferable. So he leant out and listened to *Lady Margaret*.

There is something about the noise of a locomotive working hard, the monotonous roaring rhythm of power, that can hypnotise and compel ; and it gives some people the queasy feeling at the pit of the stomach that we all feel when we are deeply moved. It is only a machine breathing ; but in another way it is a kind of music, a wonderful, deafening, savage chanting. Owen thought about it for a minute. 'I wonder whether the dragons the stories tell of ever made a noise like this ?' he was going to say ; but he decided Angus might think him light-headed. And then with a start he suddenly came to earth, and remembered that it was high time to put on some more coal.

Angus, as a practical Scot, was pleased with the success of the experiment. As they passed Hafod Eithaf he looked again at the water gauge ; the level had really only fallen very slightly, and should easily see them over the top. As they stormed over the viaduct the three labourers left off their work and gazed in wonder. So did the cottagers all the way up the hill, and when they finally blasted up on to the last lap, the long straight climbing to Garthowen, Owen could see that half the village seemed to have heard the noise from afar off and had assembled near the station to watch them go through.

'We shall have to stop here,' said Angus. 'Before we do, fill the boiler with the injector, or else the water will

36

all run forward and uncover the firebox when we go down the other side. I'll go and see about the brakes.'

They rolled over the top, and one by one the coaches nosed back on to the level. Angus shut the regulator, and they stopped at the platform. Slowly the echoes died away in the mountains.

Once again Owen made the injector work the first time. I'm getting good at this, he thought. Mr Parker and Mr Sullivan came up.

'Well, you made it, Duncan,' Mr Parker said. 'How did she go?'

'Very nicely. She was working to the limit most of the way, but she made steam for it, which is more than many another engine would have done. I was just going to set the handbrake on one of these engines; will you have yours on at the back, just to keep the couplings tight?'

'Yes, I will—I was going to in any case,' answered Mr Sullivan. 'We don't want to get out of control and deliver all this new stock to the bottom of the lake. We'll get back to the van now—go when you're ready.'

They turned back. Angus shouldered his way through the chattering crowd on the platform. Owen felt a tug on his sleeve. He turned, and recognised a friend of his, Robert Hughes, who lived near by. He was a few months younger than Owen, but they had shared a desk, and books, while they were at school. In the years since they had rather drifted apart; Robert's family lived between Hafod Eithaf and Garthowen, and they were therefore separated by distance.

'Owen, are you working on the little railway now?'

'Yes—they said they'd take me on, anyhow.'

'Liking it?'

'Yes, very much—but this is only my first day.'

'I want to, too. My father says it's all right, but my

37

mother says they won't take you till you're fifteen, which means I'll have to wait till Christmas.'

Angus broke in on the conversation. 'You're a big lad for fourteen,' he said. 'Are you sure your mother hasn't made a mistake?' and he winked solemnly. 'First come, first served, young lad, and there's no harm trying—only don't tell anybody I said so.'

Robert looked startled. 'I hadn't thought of that,' he said. 'Thank you very much—I'll try and see.' At that moment Mr Parker and Mr Sullivan climbed aboard the van and waved; Angus blew the whistle and started.

'I'll see you tomorrow, Owen!' Robert shouted as they drew away.

'Confident, isn't he?' said Angus. 'A friend of yours?'

'Yes, we went to school together,' Owen replied. After a moment he added, 'He should do all right here. He was a clever one at school: he came second in the class.'

'Did he, now?' said Angus. 'Well, that should prove something. And who came first?'

Owen flushed, and muttered that *he* had.

'Well, I'm not surprised. You can always tell the difference between a lad who did well at school and one who didn't. You'll hear a lot of loud talk later on about how men say they never learnt anything at school and how they've done better without it; but they've none of them learnt anything since, so never you believe a word of what they say.'

'I don't,' Owen answered, taking him into his confidence suddenly. 'Everybody else said they were glad when they left school, so I said I was too; but I enjoyed it, and I was sorry to go. I liked reading books and learning things.'

'Good for that. Still, this is no time to talk about such

things.  You remind me some time and I'll see if I've got any books that would interest you.'

With that the subject was dropped, and they concentrated on getting the train down the hill.  The speed was checked by the other brakes, and so Angus didn't have to use the one on *Lady Margaret* except when the grade steepened, as it did from time to time.  They saw the blue-black expanse of Llyn Gwernal ahead of them and below, and the grey roofs of the village tucked in a fold of the hills at the nearer end.  Eventually they drew into the station yard, with a prolonged whistle to attract attention.  Owen saw that the men who had been building the platform in the morning had now finished ; the platelayers had moved round the curve, and for the first time the rails stretched as far in that direction as he could see.  He was startled to notice that where the gang had been working in the morning the rails seemed to bend upwards, as if they were climbing the roof of a house.

' One in forty,' said Angus, following his gaze.  ' Steeper than anything we've climbed today.'

Mr Sullivan came up and gave Angus instructions where the various parts of the train were to be put.  *Jennie* would be the first of the new locomotives to be tried out, and so she was to go at the front of the engine shed.  The coaches would have to stay out in the open for the time being, as the carriage shed was not yet finished ; and the wagons loaded with rails and sleepers were to be left on the main line, ready to be taken up to the railhead.  ' After that you can draw the fire,' he said.  ' We shan't be needing anything more today.'

When all the shunting had been done Owen and Angus filled the coal bunkers and water tanks on *Lady Margaret* and *Jennie*, and then Angus took a long hooked rod and showed Owen how to drop the fire, by pulling out one or two firebars and raking the embers into the ashpan,

39

where they could be removed with a shovel. Fortunately Owen had let the fire burn very low, but, even so, getting it out was a very hot and choking and unpleasant job indeed. 'You can imagine what it's like getting out a big fire,' said Angus, 'and that's a waste of coal, too.'

Then *Lady Margaret* was driven into the shed, and everything was ready to be left for the night. Owen suddenly felt very tired, although it was not yet five. Angus drew some hot water from the injector overflow pipe, and they washed off the day's dirt.

'How did I do today?' asked Owen.

Angus dried his face on a towel which he had produced from somewhere before replying. 'Oh, not too badly,' he said. 'You've still got a lot to learn, but if you keep on as you've done today you'll be all right.'

'Then do you think I'll be able to stay and work here?'

'Well—very likely. But we'll see at the end of the week.'

That was a relief, for Owen was beginning to feel that things had gone too easily and smoothly to be true. Not that he had ever thought of what would happen if he failed to keep the job : that was a disaster too horrible to dream of. When he got home he lay back in the easy chair which he had never before been allowed to sit in. 'It's your father's,' his mother said, 'but you're a man, now, too, and earning money, so you had better share it with him.' As she made him a meal he told her what had happened all day ; and since she was a wise woman she didn't ask questions about the technical words he used that she didn't understand.

Owen ate, and then, somewhat less tired, went out on the farm to see if he could find his father. He found him resting at the foot of their mountain field, leaning on the stone wall and looking over the village far below.

' So there you are, lad,' he said as Owen came up. ' I was just thinking about you. How did the day go ? '

Owen repeated his story over again.

' That's good,' his father said when he had finished. ' I'm glad things seem to be going well. You know what your mother and I feel about it, don't you ? We could do with your help here, but don't worry about that—down there you've got more of a chance than we had, and if you can do better than we've done, that's all we want to see.'

They started walking back to the house.

' Mother let me sit in your chair tonight,' Owen said.

' Did she, now ? ' His father chuckled. ' Well, I can see I shall have to be sharing it with you now, indeed—for it's you who'll be the breadwinner in this house.'

## III

I<small>T</small> was the middle of the next morning before *Jennie* was ready for her fire to be lit, and while Mr Sullivan and Angus were working on her, Owen was cleaning and polishing once again. He had a lot to do : *Jennie* boasted a great deal of brass and copper work, and it was all begrimed with the dirt of the journey from Scotland. He was beginning to feel despondent at the small progress he was making when Robert Hughes appeared, and announced that he, too, had been taken on.

'Well, now you're here, take some of this rag and start cleaning,' said Owen, tasting the joys of giving orders for the first time, by virtue of his one day's seniority. Robert obeyed, and between the two of them they made better progress. By midday they had finished, and they then proceeded to inspect all three locomotives very thoroughly, clambering in, on and under them all.

Angus was loading some buckets filled with coarse, dry sand into the cab. 'We shall have to get a store of this in,' he said. 'We'll be needing it with this girl on wet days.' Robert asked why; and then Angus patiently explained how the rails became slippery when they were wet, and how it was impossible for the driving wheels to get a good grip on them without sand.

'And it's a strange paradox that the more feet a locomotive has the less likely she is to lose them,' he added. This puzzled even Owen, so eventually Angus had to explain what he meant; how when a locomotive slipped it was said to 'lose its feet', and how with six driving wheels it was possible to put more weight on the rails, and so get a better grip of them, than with four. By the time this had been explained *Jennie* had begun to make rumbling noises. Angus went into the cab to turn on the blower. Owen remembered just in time what had happened to him the day before, and stood well clear of the chimney; Robert, not having the benefit of that experience, caught most of the filthy warm water this time.

'That happened to me yesterday,' laughed Owen, throwing a clean rag at him.

'Then why didn't you warn me?'

'Oh, that would never do—you've got to learn things the hard way here.'

An hour later *Jennie* had raised steam, and all the valves and injectors had been tested. Mr Sullivan climbed into the cab, produced a long watery cry on the whistle, and opened the regulator. There was a faint hissing of steam from somewhere, otherwise nothing happened. Mr Sullivan murmured something, and opened it a little wider. Still nothing happened, except that the hissing grew a little louder. He shut it again with a puzzled expression on his face.

'Pardon me, sir,' said Angus, looking at the reversing lever, 'but she's in mid gear.'

43

'So she is,' said Mr Sullivan. 'Well, well!'

He pulled the lever over into full reverse gear and impatiently opened the regulator again, wider than before.

It was fortunate that *Jennie* was standing only a few feet from the wall at the end of the shed, otherwise the consequences might have been more serious altogether. As it was, very little damage was done. *Jennie*, with wild hissing of steam from the cylinder cocks and a bark from the exhaust, leapt forward and crashed into the wall with a noise that was heard out in the village. Her wheels spun madly before the dumbfounded Mr Sullivan could close the regulator again; but when she stopped he started to speak, and carried on for several minutes. Angus was most impressed. Later he said, 'I never thought any Sassenach had such a command of the language!' But before running out of breath Mr Sullivan had explained, with certain embellishments, that evidently Mr Pearson's brain had been so befuddled after working out his patent valve gear that he had connected up the reversing lever wrongly; a fault which he was at pains to point out violated all the canons of sound locomotive engineering.

'But ten to one she'll still go forward in fore gear,' he finished, climbing out to survey the damage. The buffers had been bent upwards slightly, but fortunately the rest of the locomotive appeared to be sound. The wall was more than two feet thick, and the only signs of the impact were two small craters and a certain amount of chipped slate. He climbed back into the cab with Angus, put the reversing lever forward, and opened the regulator very cautiously indeed. To the relief of all *Jennie* steamed sedately backward, out of the shed, and halted under the water crane. 'Thank heaven for that!' said Mr Sullivan.

After that rousing start the rest of the trials were bound to be something of an anticlimax. Once the little eccentricity of the reversing lever had been learnt, *Jennie* behaved

44

herself rather well. She rode well and made plenty of steam, though as expected she needed careful handling to avoid slipping at the starts. The three-cylinder arrangement made little difference to her behaviour ; all that was apparent was that she gave six exhaust beats for every revolution of the driving wheels instead of four, and after being accustomed to the 'ONE-two-three-four' of the other engines they all found *Jennie*'s 'One-TWO-three-four-FIVE-six' rather strange. Mr Sullivan played around with her in the yard for half an hour, and expressed qualified satisfaction ; and at half past two they coupled on to a string of empty wagons and started on the first road test. Mr Sullivan drove and Angus fired ; the two boys were allowed to come to act as messengers in case of disaster, and rode in one of the wagons. They only went as far as Hafod Eithaf, then ran round and returned ; this time Angus drove. They went rather slowly as far as Garthowen on the return journey, as Mr Sullivan feared that some of the new bearings might run hot. But they stopped at the top on the way back and felt around, and strangely enough all the bearings were cool.

'I expect the old man ran her in on his test track,' said Mr Sullivan. 'I think we'll risk it and let her run a bit down the hill.'

'Right,' said Angus, slightly disapprovingly, and they did so. As Mr Sullivan had anticipated, Pearson's patent valve gear now began to show its advantages. *Jennie* ran very freely indeed ; and this explains the fact that with only a breath of steam on going down the hill they reached a speed of thirty-five miles an hour, which of course was equivalent to more than eighty on the standard gauge. Angus was delighted, and so was Mr Sullivan ; they were, however, somewhat alarmed at the rough riding on the unsettled track at that speed, and so slowed down considerably before they reached the station. Owen and

45

Robert, travelling in an unsprung wagon, were naturally more alarmed still. They were hurled from side to side as it rocked and jolted about, and were rather bruised by the time the train stopped.

'That was a ride to remember,' said Robert. Owen felt much the same about it, but had his seniority to think of. So he said, 'Oh, it wasn't so bad. You have to learn to take these things in your stride.'

'Sorry, lads,' said Angus a few minutes later. 'I hope we didn't shake you up too much. Next time we go speeding we'll take the coaches.'

'Could she have gone any faster, do you think?' asked Owen.

'It's difficult to say, but very likely she could, on better track.'

Meanwhile Mr Sullivan was examining the way the reversing lever was connected to the valve gear. Fortunately it seemed only a small job to correct this; the trouble seemed to be due to the fact that what might be called an Intermediate Rocking Link was mounted upside down. 'We can soon straighten that out,' he said to Angus; 'but I shall write to Pearson myself and tell him that his ingenuity is too much for his factory to cope with.'

'Doubt if that'll do any good,' said Mr Parker, who had come out to see what was happening. 'Ever had a letter from him? He can hardly be called co-operative. He'll probably find some reason why the lever's better that way round, and sue you if you try to alter it.'

*Jennie* was then put away for the night, and people started to go home.

'Since we're off early the night,' said Angus, 'if you've got ten minutes to spare come round to my lodgings and have a look at some of my books.'

'Thank you very much—I'd like to,' answered Owen.

Angus was boarding at a house at the other end of the

46

village until the first terrace of quarrymen's houses was completed. The quarry company was building these, but they had agreed to let the railway company have the tenancy of several of them for its own employees, and Angus had been allotted one. As soon as he could move in, he told Owen, he would get his wife and small daughter to come down from Glasgow. But in spite of being alone, he had made his small room very comfortable, as Owen realised when he followed him into it. A large framed engraving entitled 'The Stag at Bay' hung over the fireplace, and Owen examined this with curiosity, as it was the first time he had ever seen it.

'Oh, that!' said Angus. 'The wife told me to bring it down with me, to remind me of Scotland. Anyhow, here are some of my books; have a look through them and see if there's anything you'd like to read.'

Owen sat down in front of a shelf which held about twenty-five books and started looking through them. Most of them were about railways and locomotives, and from these he selected a copy of Smiles' *Life of George Stephenson*, a book about American railways in the Civil War, which he opened at a plate showing the Railway Chase through Georgia and chose on that account, and finally a stout volume entitled *The Engineman's Concise Guide to the Locomotive*, by one Charles Pearson. He called to Angus and asked if it was the same man who had built the Gwernal Valley locomotives.

'Aye, it's the same,' Angus answered. 'He gave me a copy of that book when he sent me down here.'

When he had selected these three books Owen settled back to examine them more closely. Angus came over, looked at the ones he had chosen, and told him that he could take them home with him to read if he liked, if he promised to take care of them. Owen thanked him very much.

'The American book ought to interest you,' Angus said. 'Their Civil War was the first war which was fought with railways, and it made a great difference because they were able to move armies quickly for hundreds of miles, and keep them supplied easily. But you'd better read Mr Pearson's book first, for he's coming down next month, and if you tell him you've read it you'll get on the right side of him.'

Owen laughed, and gathered the books under his arm. 'Thank you very much for these,' he said. 'I'll let you have them back as soon as I've finished.'

'That's all right, lad. See you tomorrow morning, then.'

Owen walked home, passing Mr Parker on the way and deferentially wishing him a good evening. His younger sister saw him climbing up the path and rushed down to meet him. 'I saw you this afternoon, on the train !' she said. 'You were travelling in a truck going at a hundred miles an hour, and you didn't answer me when I called to you.'

'Didn't I ? I didn't see you—I was too busy hanging on tight.'

'Mother saw you, too, and she was very angry at them for going so fast. She said they'd come off the rails and you'd be killed.'

'Oh, dear ! Well, I'd better explain it to her.'

He went in and eventually managed to do so, but not before he had had to listen to a lecture on the stupidity of excessive speeding, and the cruelty of running the risk of being killed and bringing grey hairs to his parents' heads. However, after a few minutes things quietened down ; he ate his meal, then retired to his father's chair and read Mr Pearson on the Locomotive until it was time to go to bed.

48

## IV

*Jennie* was tried out early in June; the railway was due to be opened for public traffic between Abergwernal and Port Elwyn at the beginning of August. This meant that the intervening seven weeks were filled with great activity. All the track had been laid, but it still had to be finally levelled and aligned, and in July a hundred men were taken off the party working on the quarry extension and put on to this task. Carpenters and painters were at work on all the station buildings, and Mr Parker, among other things, had to organise the printing and stocking of tickets, waybills, time sheets, bye-laws, lists of fares and charges, all sorts of forms and tables and booklets, headed notepaper for the company's official letters to be written on, and all the varied paraphernalia necessary for running a railway, not forgetting a set of ticket clippers (beautiful shiny brass ones, each making a differently shaped hole), and half a dozen guards' whistles. Mr Sullivan in the shops supervised the fitting up of the machinery, and was nearing the end of his tether when Mr Parker suddenly produced three skilled men, borrowed or stolen from Crewe works, who proceeded in one week to make order out of the chaos which a gang of local workmen had developed in two months. Mr Sullivan muttered a song of rejoicing and thankfulness and turned his attention to getting *Lady Gwyneth* into service. Outside, a gang of contractor's men were busy installing the signals and fitting out the signal boxes, while another gang were erecting telegraph poles and stringing up wires.

All this time it was necessary to run a train every day to bring materials up from the coast, and to take down loads of slate ; for without waiting for the official opening some had already begun to come down on horseback from the quarries. These trains were usually worked by one of the two bigger engines, as Mr Sullivan didn't want *Jennie* to be used more often than was absolutely necessary. Angus drove, and Owen and Robert shared the fireman's job on alternate days. So the valley folk slowly became used to hearing the noise of the train barking up the hill, and rattling its way down the other side ; and the rooks ceased to caw whenever they heard the whistle.

Everything, in short, was going well. Mr Sullivan was pleased with progress, and decided that as long as he thought of them separately, he could view the prospect of Mr Pearson's state visit on the one hand, and the approaching inspection by the Board of Trade on the other, with equanimity. However, one morning in mid-July Mr

Parker shattered his complacency by announcing that he had just heard that both were going to arrive on the same day.

'That's a diabolical coincidence,' said Mr Sullivan. 'Can't you do anything about it?'

'Afraid not, old man—I've tried. The Board of Trade, as you know, have to be pandered to in every way, and if we asked them to come at a different time we'd probably put their backs up at once. And when I wrote to Pearson asking him if he could manage a different date, he wrote right back saying that it was impossible, and in any case he would be delighted to meet the Inspector.'

'I can imagine why.'

'Yes: he added that he would " be able to show him a thing or two."'

'Pah!' was all Mr Sullivan could reply to that, but he said it twice, and with a great deal of feeling. Then he said, 'Well, you'd better get ready to postpone the opening. I'll lay five pounds to a packet of peanuts that with Charlie Pearson demonstrating locomotives all over the place the Inspector will get a fright and declare that the opening would be attended with danger to the public.'

Still, there was, as Mr Parker pointed out, nothing to be done about it now except to hope for the best. By the beginning of the last week in July all was ready; the stations were fully equipped, and their staffs uniformed and installed, enjoying what amounted to a week's holiday with pay, as there was really very little to do before public traffic started. All the buildings shone with bright new paint, all the signals were at last in working order, and the welkin rang with the noise of the testing of the telegraph bells. On the Monday of that week Angus and Owen worked the usual daily goods train with *Jennie*, but started earlier, so that when they returned to Abergwernal they hastily recoaled and watered, and returned with a special one-coach passenger train, carrying Mr Parker and Mr Sullivan, to meet the Inspector and Mr Pearson, who were both arriving on the same main-line train. They reached Port Elwyn in good time ; early, in fact, so that they had the mortification of standing outside the station at the home signal for the first time, because the signalman had gone to have a cup of tea.

While they were waiting in the station Mr Sullivan walked up and down the platform in an agitated manner, for that day he had received a letter from a friend who was also an engineer, and who had had dealings with the Inspector who was coming. *Colonel Richards was one of the most fearsome gentlemen I have ever been under*, the letter said. *He is extremely thorough and by no means disposed to overlook any minor infringement, or even bending, of the rules.* And although Mr Sullivan knew that it would be a clever man who could find anything to complain of in the Gwernal Valley's equipment, that did not prevent him from worrying. Perhaps Colonel Richards *was* a clever man.

They had been ready and waiting for twenty minutes when the local from Chester rolled in, no later than usual. Owen and Angus had both been busily polishing the last specks of dirt off *Jennie*'s immaculate paint and brasswork, and now could find nothing more to do than lean out of the cab and watch the official party come walking up the platform towards them.

Colonel Richards looked exactly the type of man Mr Sullivan had most feared. Tall and thin, with a pale, narrow face and prominent nose, he was carrying a briefcase which was obviously bulging with Parliamentary plans and specifications, and little black books in which all the deviations from the authorised line would be noted down. He spoke little, but strode up to *Jennie* and looked her over with a critical, professional, and slightly disapproving eye. Nor were Mr Sullivan or Mr Parker greatly relieved by meeting Charles Pearson in the flesh. He was a very different man indeed : a large, ruddy, bearded Scot, with a loud voice which rose to a shout whenever anybody disagreed with him. The little party gathered round *Jennie* while their luggage was stowed in the guard's compartment ; Mr Pearson, after exchanging a few words with Angus, warning him that he intended to do some driving the next day ('Whether young Parker likes it or not,' he added in a slightly louder voice, so that Mr Parker could hear), turned to the Inspector and pointed out to him the beauties of his patent valve gear.

Before they started Mr Sullivan found an opportunity to warn Angus that they had had trouble already with the Inspector, because he had mentioned in a letter that he did not see how a speed of as much as thirty miles an hour could possibly be safe on so narrow a gauge as two feet. So Angus was very cautious indeed, and did not go faster than twenty. Even so, Colonel Richards was observed to look nervously out of the window from time to time, and mutter something about speed.

As a result of this the atmosphere in the coach was far from comfortable as they discussed the arrangements for the next day.

'I understand that you would like to walk the whole length of the line, sir,' said Mr Sullivan.

'That is so,' said the Colonel. 'A great many of my brethren would be satisfied to travel over it in a train. But in my view such a cursory examination would make it only too easy for the company to conceal some improper practice.'

Mr Sullivan winced. Mr Parker went on, after an uncomfortable silence :

'In that case, I thought that it would be easiest, if you agreed, that you should walk down from Abergwernal, with Mr Sullivan and myself, in the morning ; and in the afternoon we could send a train down to Port Elwyn to fetch you back.'

'That would be satisfactory, indeed. But of course I do not guarantee to be able to finish the inspection in one day. Under certain circumstances——'

Mr Sullivan winced again. 'Quite, quite,' Mr Parker interrupted. 'But in any case we would have to send a train down to bring you back, so if necessary it can easily stop half-way and pick you up.'

'That seems a very good plan,' put in Mr Pearson. 'I would like to travel on at least one of my engines while I am down here, and that would make a good opportunity. That is,' he added, turning and glowering at that unhappy man, 'if Mr Sullivan doesn't mind.'

Mr Sullivan muttered disconsolately that he would be only too delighted to arrange it.

'In that case I think we can regard the matter as settled,' said Mr Pearson, looking fiercely round to see if anybody would be rash enough to make an objection. But even the Colonel hardly cared to do so, and the conversation turned in other directions.

After an uneventful journey the train arrived at Abergwernal, and while Angus and Owen were putting the engine away the information was telegraphed down the line that the usual goods train would not run the next day, in order that the inspection might not be disturbed, and that a special passenger train would be run during the afternoon to bring the Inspector back.

In the shed Angus was shaking his head in a dismal manner. Owen asked him what the matter was.

'Och, lad, it's a pity that Mr Pearson and the Inspector are here together. I can see that they don't like each other, and I've seen that fey look in Mr Pearson's eyes too often not to know that no good will come of it.'

'Why, what do you think he'll do?'

54

'Well, I've got to let him drive tomorrow. He doesn't know the road, but that won't stop him wanting to see how fast she'll go—and probably he'll want to do it with the Inspector aboard, just for the devilment of it.'

'Would it be any good if I had the handbrake on lightly?' suggested Owen, hoping that this would be helpful.

Angus chuckled. 'No, lad, I don't think that would do. He knows too much about locomotives not to notice that.'

'Then there's not much else we can do, is there?'

'No, that's the pity of it. I don't see what there is to be done, except for us to sit back and keep our fingers crossed.'

With that they finished putting *Jennie* away, and went home. That night Mr Sullivan hardly slept at all, anxiously wondering whether there was any minor detail he had forgotten. Mr Parker lay awake for some time, glumly pondering the most suitable wording for the announcement that 'Owing to causes beyond the Company's control, the opening of the railway would be indefinitely postponed.' Colonel Richards sat up very late reading railway accident reports, and Charles Pearson dreamt happily of newer, bigger, faster locomotives emerging in greater and greater numbers from his works, and of the larger and larger profits which he would make as a result.

The next day was wet in the morning, but cleared up at midday. Mr Parker, observing the rain pouring down outside his bedroom window as he opened one bleary eye, decided that he didn't really want to walk the line with the Inspector, and so over breakfast he made a number of shabby excuses to Mr Sullivan, leaving him to face the ordeal alone. The Inspector was up early, and demanded the key of the Abergwernal signal box before breakfast. Mr Sullivan leapt out of bed when he heard this, dressed, and rushed round to find the Colonel happily pulling levers to and fro. 'Testing the interlocking,' he said. But much to his surprise he found the installation beyond complaint, and in an unguarded moment said as much to Mr Sullivan, who took new life at once and showed the Inspector over the yard and sheds with a great deal more confidence than he had felt for several days. After breakfast they started walking down the line, wrapped up in oilskins. They stopped to examine every bridge and culvert, and from time to time the Colonel flung himself flat on the sleepers to examine whether the rails were level, or produced a tape measure to check on their accuracy to gauge. At each station the same detailed examination was carried out, and the staff inspected as if they were on parade at Aldershot. But never once did the Inspector find anything to note down in his little black book, and as the day went by Mr Sullivan's cheerfulness increased. Contrary to all prediction, they reached Port Elwyn just before five o'clock, and while the stationmaster was despatched to enquire whether their train had already left Abergwernal, they sat down in the waiting-room and ate sandwiches together almost as if they were friends.

'Yes, I think things are in quite reasonable shape here,' said the Colonel, happy because he had found a pile of salmon sandwiches, which he very much liked. 'Your track doesn't seem to be bad at all. I just want to hold some tests with heavy trains up and down your hill, and if they are satisfactory I think I shall have no difficulty in passing the line. Subject, of course, to a speed limit of fifteen miles an hour, which is all that can be regarded as safe on so narrow a gauge.'

Mr Sullivan was too pleased at the first part of this pronouncement to be greatly upset at the second; so while he ate the cheese sandwiches which the Inspector had left for him, they conversed quite amiably about fishing prospects in the lake until the train arrived.

# V

AFTER Mr Sullivan and the Inspector left the weather began to improve. Mr Parker was relieved to see this; it meant that he now had only one worry: Charles Pearson. That gentleman, however, spent a very peaceful morning examining the locomotives and rolling stock on his own, and the only time Mr Parker met him he was greeted with nothing worse than praise for the idea of carrying standard-gauge wagons on transporter trucks, admiration for the amount of money which would be saved by avoiding transhipment, and only nine ways in which the methods used could be improved upon. He made a show of noting down Mr Pearson's suggestions, promised him that he would see that they were taken up, and escaped. In the early afternoon all was peaceful, too: *Jennie* was getting up steam, Owen was gently chopping firewood, and the energetic Mr Pearson was out of the way, walking up the line towards the quarries to see how construction was getting on. But at three o'clock the fun began.

By that time *Jennie* had raised steam, and had been coaled, watered and oiled. When Mr Pearson returned from his walk he saw that she was ready for him to test, so he went up to Angus and told him what he proposed to do.

' I've just been walking up towards the quarries,' he said. ' I see that they've got the track laid for about a mile up the hill, so I want to try this locomotive out on the gradient, with a load. We'll take four coaches and that rake of trucks for a start, and see how she manages that. Let me drive.'

Angus gave up his place on the driver's side and stood in the middle of the cab. Mr Pearson opened the firedoor and examined the fire, which was low, since Owen had not expected that much steam would be needed for some time. He was about to say that a larger fire was wanted, but Owen, being a smart lad, forestalled him, grabbed the shovel, and had started baling coal into the firebox before he could speak. Clouds of black smoke poured from the chimney, and the needle of the pressure gauge began to move.

After a few minutes the train was ready. With a long pull on the whistle, Mr Pearson opened up, and with an awful snatch on the couplings *Jennie* started for the hill. But in spite of Angus's fears he wasn't such a very bad driver after all ; with such an energetic start *Jennie* slipped once or twice, but he controlled her competently. They were doing almost twenty miles an hour when they came to the foot of the hill, and rolling rather badly on the newly laid, unfinished track. As they started to climb Owen could feel the engine lifting. However, her designer

58

had rather overestimated her capabilities. Owen provided him with all the steam he could use, but the train was too heavy. Although the rails were dry now after the morning's rain, *Jennie* soon began to slip when Mr Pearson worked her hard, and when he eased her back slightly to stop the slipping the speed slowly fell. For all the noise she made, her exhaust gradually became slower and more laboured, and after half a mile she finally came to a stand, wrapped in a cloud of steam.

'Well, well, too bad indeed !' said Mr Pearson. 'Never mind ; we'll leave the wagons behind and see how she can manage the coaches.'

Owen dismounted and ran back to uncouple the wagons, not forgetting to pin down their brakes first. When he returned to the cab Mr Pearson tried to start with the lightened load, but *Jennie* would have none of it. She would nudge forward, and then the driving wheels would spin helplessly, showers of sparks would shoot up into the air, and the train would remain standing in exactly the same place. Angus handed Owen the bucket of sand which he had previously stowed away in a corner of the cab against this emergency, and told him to go and throw some under the wheels. With this assistance, and with Owen sitting on the front buffer beam to repeat the dose if any further slipping occurred, *Jennie* at last got away.

There was half a mile more to go before they reached the end of the track ; and since Owen had been up the hill several times before with trains carrying track materials, he knew exactly how far it stretched and had no fear of rounding a curve to find the rails missing. But it was just as well that he kept a good lookout forward, because they had not gone a quarter of a mile before, round just such a blind curve, there appeared a trolley which four plate-layers were riding down the hill. For a fraction of a second Owen stared at the four of them, and they stared back ;

then he flung himself off the engine on to the side of the cutting, while at the same time the platelayers bundled themselves off the trolley in quick succession and rolled down the hill on the other side. An instant later, before anybody had time to shout, let alone do anything to avert the collision, there was a mighty crash, and the air flew with fragments. A large cast-iron wheel, on half an axle, whistled past Owen's ear as he lay in the ditch, and buried itself in the bank above his head. *Jennie* stopped at once, and as Owen got up and dusted himself, he found he was standing opposite her cab, in which Charles Pearson, the great Scottish locomotive magnate, was shaking with laughter.

'Man, did ye see those gangers unload? Like a pack of scared rabbits!' he said after a pause for breath, and then started off laughing again. Angus looked as white as a sheet, but was reassured when he looked down into the ravine and saw the four platelayers climbing slowly up again. Evidently nobody had been hurt, which was very lucky.

Quite understandably the Irishmen, when they arrived, were disposed to be quarrelsome, and their leader started an oration on the subject of what were they doing with a locomotive up there at that time of day without warning anybody; but on recognising Mr Pearson standing in the cab he found the wind taken out of his sails, and stopped and began to cough in an apologetic manner. This was a pity in a way, and certainly saved him nothing, for Mr Pearson counter-attacked. Pulling out a large gold watch on the end of a long chain, and glaring sternly at the four, he announced that the time was 3.45 p.m.

'And what time did you tell me that you finished work?' he demanded. There was no intelligible reply, so he added, 'Five o'clock, I think you said?'

'Yes, sorr, but——'

'There are no "buts". If you were to finish work at five o'clock, what are you doing leaving it at a quarter to four? You were each robbing the company of more than an hour's work, weren't you? Time for which you would have been paid money? Do you realise that this was no more than theft? And do you realise that you can be sent to prison for theft? What is more, through leaving work early you were very nearly killed, to say nothing of the fact that in your wickedness you wantonly damaged the Company's property . . .' and more in the same strain. The platelayers were evidently relieved when he stopped and told them to clear up the mess.

'Wicked old man, isn't he!' muttered Angus. 'He knows perfectly well he should have warned them he was bringing the train up.'

Fortunately *Jennie* was very little damaged by the impact, beyond a few small dents and a certain amount of scratched paint, and after a brief look to make sure that nothing more serious had happened, Mr Pearson decided to return to Abergwernal, because it was drawing on for teatime. So he released the brake, and they began to roll down the hill. Now, of course, the coaches were in front, so they didn't have a very good view of the line ahead. It was therefore unfortunate that nobody remembered about the trucks they had left behind. Although they were only doing about ten miles an hour, they stopped very abruptly with a horrible crunching sound.

Owen and Angus exchanged glances as they climbed down and went to examine the wreckage. As soon as they were out of earshot Angus said that this was worse even than he had feared already, and the Lord preserve them all but there was still the Inspector's trip ahead of them.

This was a rather worse smash than the last. Seven wagons were derailed; four of them had been thrown down the hill quite clear of the line, and the other three were lying at various angles to the track. All were more or less damaged, but repairable. The end platform of the last coach had been shattered, and the floor was bent upwards in a curve, rather gracefully if one ignored the jagged splinters of crushed wood. To cap it all off, one bogie had been derailed.

However, one of the advantages of a narrow-gauge railway is that its wrecks are very easily cleared up; in fact, with a little bit of luck it is possible for all traces of a mishap to be cleared away by the time the first sightseers arrive, when the standard reply to their questions becomes, 'Accident? What accident?' With the assistance of the four gangers, who arrived on the scene on foot a few minutes later, order was soon restored. The wagons which would run were rerailed, and the others tipped on to the side of the cutting, out of the way. Half an hour's work with the jacks had the last coach back on the track, and a few minutes before five o'clock a slightly battered train, driven by a completely unabashed Pearson, backed down slowly into Abergwernal station. Mr Parker stood on the platform, and looked glumly at the crumpled coach and wagons as they rolled past.

'I'm glad you're back,' he said to Mr Pearson. 'I was just going to go up and look for you.'

'Ah, yes, we had a spot of bother up the line. No damage, though—the engine's quite all right, bar a couple of dents in the paintwork. I suppose we ought to be going down soon to collect that inspector chappie, eh?'

Mr Pearson then drove on and proceeded to shunt the battered wagons and coach into a siding. Owen went with him to do the uncoupling, and Angus went into the signal box to change the points. Mr Parker followed him in.

'Can you tell me exactly what happened?' he asked.

Angus told him. Mr Parker growled when he heard

what had happened to the platelayers, and said that it was lucky that they weren't killed. He groaned when he heard that some damaged wagons still stood by the lineside, and then went off to find the leader of the three men from Crewe, who were just going off duty. By the time Mr Pearson had finished shunting, and *Jennie*, hauling only one coach, had left for Port Elwyn, they were still shaking their heads and stroking their beards over the wreckage.

Mr Pearson rode on the engine this time, while Angus drove ; he said that he would drive coming back, when he knew the line a bit better. And so they had an uneventful run down to the coast, and drew into the platform just as Colonel Richards finished the last salmon sandwich.

After a few minutes they were once again ready to leave. The Colonel decided that he felt rather too stiff after his long walk to ride on the footplate, and said that that could wait till he carried out his braking tests next day. Owen was told to travel in the coach, as Mr Pearson said he wanted more room in the cab. Mr Sullivan and the Inspector sat together, talking.

'Pity the Colonel funked coming on the engine,' said Mr Pearson, as he opened the regulator. 'Never mind— let's see how much we can shake him up in the coach.'

Angus gave a strained smile.

It was obvious after a few seconds what Mr Pearson was up to. *Jennie*, with so light a load, had pretty rapid acceleration in any case, but he drove her very hard indeed right from the start. They bounced and swayed uncomfortably going over the last turnout in the station, accelerated rapidly along the section beside the main line, heeled over and took the curve which turned them towards the distant hills at a good forty miles an hour, and then shot over the junction with the harbour branch with such a rattle and crash that Angus thought for a moment that the worst had happened. But they steadied again, and as they entered

63

on the long straight stretch to Castle Rock Pearson opened out fully. Fast as they were going already, *Jennie* surged forward again perceptibly, and as they gathered still more speed Angus, hardened engineman as he was, stood on the bouncing footplate, hung on tight, shut his eyes and prayed.

But Angus's alarm was as nothing to the consternation of the passengers. As they tore round the long curve Mr Sullivan and the Colonel both slid helplessly along their seats, snatched up by centrifugal force, and landed simultaneously with a painful bump on the floor. Mr Sullivan picked himself up, dashed into the guard's compartment, was thrown to the floor again as they went through the harbour junction, caught hold of a red flag which stood in a holder on the wall, and thrust it out of the window. He was wasting his time, as he later admitted ; Angus didn't dare lean out of the cab to look back, and in any case had his eyes shut, and Mr Pearson didn't see the flag, and wouldn't have taken any notice even if he had, no doubt. After a minute or so without visible result, he thrust his arm far out of the window and waved the flag harder than ever ; and it was at once carried away by the rushing wind.

He limped back into the first-class compartment and started to apologise to the Inspector. 'This is perfectly outrageous !' he said. 'I must apologise to you, and I can only say that Mr Pearson is *not* a Company servant, but is merely taking a most shameful advantage of his privileged position.'

The Inspector was holding his stop-watch, and had his eye out of the window, watching for the next quarter-mile post. As it flashed past he clicked his watch and exclaimed :

'Eighteen seconds ! Upon my soul, fifty-one miles an hour ! This is remarkable, truly remarkable ! And how steadily the coach is riding now !'

Mr Sullivan suddenly noticed that this was true ; along

64

the straight track their motion was much quieter. True, it was difficult to stand upright without holding on to something, but the unsteadiness was no longer so alarming. Rather thankfully he noticed that the Colonel did not seem to be angry, as he had assumed he would be, but merely incredulous. 'I can't believe it!' he kept repeating, and took out his watch again. The next quarter-mile was covered at an average of fifty-seven miles an hour.

Owen was the only person on the train, besides Mr Pearson, who felt no fear at all. He stood on the end platform of the coach, watching the rails come thudding out from under him, and go flying off into the distance, and listening to the roaring and clicking of the wheels and the steady, low purring of the locomotive. He remembered seeing the Irish Mail coming rushing through Port Elwyn a short while before at fifty miles an hour, and thinking that they would never go so fast on the Gwernal Valley; yet here they were going faster!

Back on the footplate Angus felt *Jennie* steady under his feet, and realised that they must have passed over the soft, marshy ground near the river. The going wouldn't be so bad now. So he opened his eyes again, tried not to look at the country flashing by at such a speed, and shovelled some coal on the fire. Mr Pearson was so pleased with the splendid way in which his machine was behaving and so busy keeping a lookout ahead that he had no time to notice anything else. He was conscious that, having reached firmer ground, *Jennie* was starting to gain speed again, and he felt that the last ounce had not yet been extracted from her, when he suddenly realised that they had reached the hills. Castle Rock station was already in sight, and just beyond it lay the sharp curve which brought the railway into the woods. 'Certainly we won't take it at this speed,' he said, and regretfully shut off steam and started to apply the brakes. 'However, now I've got a good idea of what she'll do, and I'll be able to build others like her with confidence.'

The rest of the journey was comparatively tame. Not surprisingly, as soon as they slowed down, the stink of scorched oil drifted into the cab ; so they stopped at Hafod Eithaf to discover where it came from, and found the axle-box on a leading wheel had run hot. However, this was easy to reach and fill with new oil, and after a wait of a few minutes Mr Pearson decided that it could be trusted as far as Abergwernal. So after that speed was moderate, and Mr Sullivan collected no more bruises. Angus gradually collected his wits, and by the time they got back to the shed he was laughing heartily and claiming he had enjoyed every minute of the run. Mr Pearson and Owen could both say the same thing, and mean it as well ; which left only Mr Sullivan and the Colonel.

But by the evening even these two had recovered themselves sufficiently not to feel too alarmed about their experience. The most remarkable thing was that after a splendid dinner, washed down with vintage wines (all paid for by the Company), Colonel Richards unbuttoned himself so far as to say, ' Fine little railway you've got here ! Jolly fine ! ' and announced his determination to make the speed limit thirty, instead of fifteen, miles an hour.

The next day the Inspector conducted his braking trials, and was satisfied after due experiment and making one or two minor suggestions. He therefore issued his edict of approval for the line's opening, and the next day both he and Mr Pearson departed in the very odour of good fellow-ship. Strange though it would have seemed to him a few days before, Mr Sullivan not only shook hands when they made their farewell, but went down to Port Elwyn to see them off. Mr Parker tore up his draft announcement about the postponement of the opening and composed another, in accordance with the terms of which the line from Port

Elwyn to Abergwernal was opened for public traffic at the beginning of the next week. The first passenger train was hauled by *Lady Gwyneth*; all the coaches were attached, and all were packed full.

The great banquet luncheon, with five hundred guests, was held in a big marquee at Abergwernal. After the meal a great many people made speeches to which nobody paid very much attention, but which were all applauded a great deal. Among these were the Chairman of the Directors himself, a great fat bushy-bearded man come all the way from London for that very purpose, who talked of the railway and the prosperity it would bring to the countryside, meaning the shareholders and especially himself; and the Lord Lieutenant of the County, a tall thin Welshman with a hooked nose and whining voice, who talked of the railway and the blessings it would bring to the shareholders, meaning the ratepayers; and numbers of other gentry whose speeches were mostly as undistinguished as they were indistinguishable. After singing a patriotic song and giving three lusty cheers, the gathering broke up. The caterers who had supplied the feast counted the breakages and totted up the bill, and reflected that on the whole they had known wilder opening days, including one when the inaugural train ran off the rails. 'But this is a much better-run railway,' said Mr Parker, overhearing the head waiter making this remark. The latter, not liking to be snubbed, hastily added ten pounds to the bill, but Mr Parker made out the cheque like a gentleman.

'Didn't go too badly at all,' he remarked to Mr Sullivan that night.

'No,' replied the other. 'And now we can settle down to do some real work.'

## VI

AFTER the opening day the railway began to earn its living. With a timetable to be kept, something of the free and easy atmosphere of the early days disappeared. Although for the first few years there were only three or four trips scheduled in each direction every day, they provided a long day's work for one engine, and its crew were on duty from half-past six in the morning till nearly seven at night. Very often a second engine would be steamed and used to bring a special train of supplies and materials up to the men who were still working on the line to the quarries. This meant that sometimes there had to be two drivers, so one of the Crewe men took the job on. These men had irritated Angus considerably by saying how much easier it must be driving a little Gwernal Valley locomotive than a big London and North Western one; but this song ceased abruptly after one of them had tried his hand at the regulator for the first time, with results almost as ignominious as those attending Mr Pearson's venture up the quarry line.

On Sundays, which were now the only days when they were both free, Owen and Robert would sometimes walk up to the quarries, to see how the extension of the railway, and the uncovering of new seams and workings of slate, were progressing. In the evening they would often visit Angus, who was leading a quiet domesticated life now that his wife and small daughter had arrived; and, sitting round the fire they would talk, or rather mostly listen to him talking, on all subjects, from politics, and the clever way in which Disraeli had dished Gladstone, to marine steam engines and the vexed problem of paddle-wheel versus propeller.

But perhaps the first change that the railway brought to the valley was the transformation of the village. With the multitude of new houses it was several times bigger, and it had also changed its character. It was now definitely a quarrymen's village, and not a farmer's one. Streets (some of them) had been paved; chapels, shops, and a new school appeared. After a few months nearly all the ground between the lake on one side, the mountains on another, and the railway on the third, had been built over, and nearly two thousand people began to call Abergwernal 'home'.

Mr Sullivan's chief preoccupation now that the passenger service was running was to see that the works on the quarry extension were finished as quickly as possible; but there was still much to be done. The building of the first mile and a half was relatively easy, and the track had been laid by the end of August; the rails already climbed high on the shoulders of the hills, overlooking the lake, and then turned away and into the mountains up a narrow side valley. Here the difficult part began. The railway was climbing as hard as it could, but the floor of the valley rose faster. In order to gain height the line turned sharply into the hillside and plunged into a long curved tunnel. This was proving to be Mr Sullivan's biggest problem, since it was a tricky job to ensure that the two headings met inside the mountain; rather like twisting two corkscrews into opposite ends of a cork so that the tips touched inside. Then it emerged, once again overlooking the lake and running beside its previous course, but now nearly fifty feet higher and facing in the opposite direction. It then slewed itself round on to a great stone viaduct, which carried it over the lower line and shot it straight into another tunnel on the opposite side of the valley. In this it seemed to lose all sense of direction, and twisted and turned underground so that when it finally emerged once more into the open air it found to its dismay that it was heading directly away from the quarries, and that its previous convulsions, and beyond them the lake and the village, lay straight in front and below. However, its wanderings were nearly at an end; and after doubling back on itself yet again, it eventually wound on to a level acre entirely surrounded by large raw gashes in the hills—the main quarry yard. It was always with a feeling of relief that the end of the line was reached; the platelayers, when they got there, were sick and tired of sawing little bits off the ends of rails to make them fit on the insides of curves; drivers, firemen and locomotives were all exhausted and needed to get their breath back; and in another way so were the passengers, half stifled in the smoky tunnels.

But at the beginning of 1877 it was still too early for Mr Sullivan to lay down his completed task and return to London. The track had been laid through the first tunnel and across the viaduct, but there it came to another dead end. Relays of navvies were working night and day to complete the second tunnel, but in the middle of it they had found a hard seam of granite which wore away their drills almost as fast as it was worn away itself, and seemed impervious to explosive. Everything else was ready by the end of February, but it was not until June that the headings finally met. Suddenly released, the track leapt forward, and the last mile into the quarry yard was laid in three days.

On the third day Owen and Angus were bringing up materials with *Jennie*. By noon it became fairly certain that the rails would reach the yard before night, and excitement gradually mounted. People collected from nowhere ; as the rails gradually neared a great boulder some twelve feet high which the ingenious surveyor had decided to use as a buffer stop, a crowd of onlookers seemed almost to rise up out of the ground. By half past four more than a hundred were gathered round to watch the platelayers install the last set of points ; and at five o'clock Angus drove *Jennie* slowly forward until she bumped into the boulder and stopped. There was a loud cheer from the crowd ; but *Jennie* outdid them all. Angus motioned Owen to hold down the whistle cord ; he turned the blower on hard, and opened the cylinder cocks and blew steam through them. The din went on from all sides until everybody was hoarse ; the railway was complete at last. Then everybody loaded themselves on to the train, just as if they had been invited, and *Jennie* wound the long string of trucks, each one overloaded with people, back down the hill and through the tunnels to the village. The only people left behind were three old shepherds on horseback, for whom there wasn't really room.

Well, thought Owen, this isn't really a proper opening day—no speeches, no banquets—nothing at all. And then he thought again. All those ceremonies had been just a party; great fun, perhaps, but all the most important people then had been from other places, and to them the Gwernal Valley was just another railway. They weren't specially interested in us, he thought; they'll probably never come back, most of them. But it's our railway, not theirs—and it's good that we should be the only people there to cheer when it is finished. We're the only people who really care.

Some of the platelayers and navvies were busy for a couple of months after that evening, tidying up generally, and laying in sidings and inclines to the various quarry workings; but the whole railway was put into regular use a few days later, and the alien workmen started to trickle home, in twos and threes, at once. Most of the valley people were glad to see them go.

# PART TWO

I

AND so three years went by. One by one the newly built
houses in the village and up in the quarries were filled by
men coming from all over North Wales to work. Slowly
the grass grew over the raw brown slopes of the cuttings
and embankments on the railway, and they ceased to look
like an angry weal cutting along the valley. The rising
tide of the Industrial Revolution had at last reached into
this remote corner of Britain, and had changed the face
of things so completely and in so short a time that the old
valley folk looked back on the days when there were only
a handful of houses, when everybody knew everybody else,
and when there were more sheep than people, as if they
had just woken from a dream.

75

Mr Sullivan had left, but Mr Parker still managed the railway. Now he presided over the quarry as well, since by some complicated transaction the railway company had obtained control over the quarry or the quarry company had obtained control over the railway; the finances were so involved that only a Chancery Judge could have told which. And with the opening of the line to the quarries there was a great increase in the amount of traffic on the railway, and more changes in the way it was worked.

Every day enough slate was produced to make two trainloads, and with the growth of the village the passenger and general goods traffic had swollen as well. On most weekdays it was still possible for one locomotive to do all the work, but on Saturdays nearly everybody would want to travel to the coast, and then they always had to use two. One would be kept busy hauling all the Saturdays-only passenger trains, and the other would have a rather easier time working the goods.

Owen quickly grew used to seeing these throngs of people crowding the station platforms; to the sight of fifty or sixty empty slate trucks dragging along in a twisting, unwilling chain behind a fussing locomotive; to hauling transporter trucks carrying standard-gauge wagons which towered above the little engine which pulled them, and to the black, wet, thundering, suffocating tumult as they climbed through the tunnels, where you had to breathe through a rag to keep out the fumes, and where the sudden emergence into light and air again was each time a thankful deliverance. But though the novelty wore off all this in time, the fascination remained.

He soon realised that each of the three locomotives had its own character, just as any three people would have. *Lady Margaret* and *Lady Gwyneth* were sisters, though, and their likenesses were more apparent than their differences; but the differences were there, and you learnt to know them

76

in time. But *Jennie* was something else again. She seemed to behave as if her record-breaking on that never-to-be-forgotten run with Mr Pearson had gone to her head. She bore only a distant family resemblance to the other two ; smaller and lighter, she was never expected to haul the same loads, and usually worked on the passenger trains. This meant that she did not go through the tunnels very often, and so it was easier to keep her clean and polished ; which seemed to add to her skittishness. Now and then, however, she would disgrace herself, and sometimes on wet days, when the rails were slippery, she would completely lose her footing, and for all her efforts and excited shooting of sparks high into the air, she would slither to a standstill on the gradient, and Owen or Robert would have to climb out and sit on the buffer beam, sprinkling sand on the rails. After this had happened a few times Mr Parker lost patience and ordered sandboxes, controlled from the cab, to be fitted, and this cured most of the trouble. But the worst disgrace of all was during Mr Sullivan's last week, when something happened to the valve gear for the middle cylinder, and it started working in opposition to the other two. Crippled like this, there was nothing for it but to have her ignominiously towed home by *Lady Gwyneth*. Mr Sullivan said, 'I knew it would happen sooner or later, and I should have known it would happen before I left' (which was a milder comment than everybody had expected). It took two days to put the trouble right ; and when he returned home and his small son presented him with a collection of puzzles made out of bits of bent wire he was not as grateful as he should have been. *Jennie* was of course thoroughly humbled, which was no doubt good for her soul, if she had one.

The winters passed uneventfully enough. There was snow, but usually it didn't stay on the ground for any length of time except up in the mountains, and was not thick enough to cause very much disturbance. After one blizzard a drift five feet deep formed in the cutting at the higher end of the second tunnel. Luckily this was on a Saturday morning, when there were two locomotives in steam, so the second one spent a busy morning charging through the drift. But it was very cold, and Owen found another reason to be glad of his choice of a career, because it was always warm in the cab, and after being frozen through outside it, he could soon thaw out again.

One Friday evening some months after the blizzard, as Angus was locking up the engine-shed and starting to go home, he called to Owen.

'Lad, you've been on the engines for nearly three years now, and you've done well enough as a fireman. I'm going to let you drive the goods tomorrow—it's time you learnt how, in case one of us falls sick. You should have learnt enough by now from watching me to know what to do. D'you think you can do it?'

'Yes, I think so—thank you very much.'

'Right, then. But don't forget it's a great responsibility. And don't go blathering about it all over the town either —I doubt Mr Parker wouldn't like it if he knew.'

Owen was now lodging in the village with his elder sister, whose husband was a quarryman. Over the meal he mentioned what Angus had said.

'Does that mean you'll be driving us up to the quarry?' asked her husband.

'I expect so,' Owen answered.

'Well, don't jolt us out of our seats, then. Those new workmen's coaches are crowded enough already without us being flung into each other's laps. When that great Scotsman does it there's nothing we can do, and he just gets up and swears at us in Gaelic when we complain.'

Owen remembered that occasion, and laughed. 'I'll ask him to teach me some too,' he said.

78

'I'll warn the boys to expect a rough trip, anyhow.'

Next morning Owen had to get up at five to light the engine, as usual. Angus had made it clear that he did not propose to do this himself. He returned for breakfast, and at six, with three-quarters of an hour to go before the train was due out, he returned to start the day's work in earnest. But Angus was sitting on the window-ledge doing nothing.

'Good morning. Don't forget you've still got to oil round her,' he said as Owen came in. Owen gulped. He hadn't thought of that; of course, it was the driver's job, but somehow he had left it out of his calculations.

'It's all right—I haven't forgotten,' he lied. He set about the job, working methodically all the way round the locomotive, and trying not to forget anything. After coming back to his starting-point, he unbent and stood up; but just in time he saw Angus looking at him with a beady eye, and suddenly realised he had forgotten the trailing-wheel axle-boxes. This omission repaired, he put the oilcans on the shelf in the cab and told Angus they were ready.

'You very nearly weren't,' said the other, clambering down, 'but you are now.'

Owen had driven each of the engines before, but only round the shed and yard, while nobody except Robert was about. Anyhow, the feel of the regulator was not so entirely strange as it had been the first time, when he nearly derailed *Lady Gwyneth* on some catch points (which would have got him into very hot water indeed), and he assembled the train, seven little four-wheeled workmen's coaches (mere boxes that had been delivered a little while before, and were not considered fit even for third-class passengers on the public trains), and twenty or so empty slate trucks, with the brake van bringing up the rear, and ran it into the station. The quarrymen were waiting on the platform

79

when the train drew up, and with a scuffle and slamming of doors were aboard it in a few seconds. The guard waved his flag.

'Now! Just see how smoothly you can start them,' said Angus. 'Right away.'

With infinite care Owen slowly eased open the regulator, and *Lady Margaret* started to move so gently that even when they had gone far enough to take all the slack out of the couplings, the wheels were still hardly turning at all.

'How's that?' asked Owen, as they started to gather speed for the rush at the hill.

'Not bad, in a way,' answered Angus; 'but if you take as long as that every time you start you're going to lose the devil of a lot of time.'

It was the first time Owen had driven an engine on a train, and so he had to act more or less by guesswork until he got the feel of the load. He experimented to see what the effects of having the reversing lever in different positions were, and saw how in full gear *Lady Margaret* would bellow away, making an enormous noise, but how the level of water in the boiler would start to drop; how that with it in a middle notch the noise would be less, but that they would continue at a comfortable speed and the water level did not go down too fast to be replaced; and how, with the lever brought right back towards the centre, the feeling of easy progress would vanish; *Lady Margaret* would start to wheeze in a strangled manner and the speed would fall alarmingly. That was a brief experiment: the effects were too violent. 'No, lad, you don't do that when you're climbing a mountain,' said Angus.

In the first tunnel *Lady Margaret* started to slip, as she nearly always did with a heavy load, but Owen was ready for her and managed to keep her under control, although not without a certain amount of nervousness. They seemed to take a trebly long time to go through the second tunnel, but when the blessed spot of light appeared round the curve they seemed to be going no slower than usual. They swung round and faced the mountains for the final climb, and a few minutes later ran into the yard. Owen heaved a sigh of relief as he shut the regulator and they coasted into the station ; he grabbed a piece of cotton waste and wiped his forehead. Suddenly he remembered the brake ; they were still going too fast to stop without it, so he reached for the steam-brake lever and opened it.

A steam-brake can be a tricky thing at the best of times, and it was really hardly fair of Angus to expect Owen to handle it properly for the first time with a train. At any rate they stopped as if they had run into a brick wall, and as each of the coaches bumped up in succession behind them there were noises of falling men and oaths. A minute or so later, as the workmen streamed past the cab, some of them limping and rubbing themselves, Owen crouched out of sight in the far corner, while Angus leant out above the crowd, smiling a broad Scots smile and wishing everybody a good morning as if nothing at all had happened. When the last casualty had limped off to work he turned to Owen, but only said, ' I think you need a bit of practice with that brake.' Owen agreed with him.

Their next job was to place the empty coaches in a siding, where they would stay until the workmen came back in the afternoon. Then they had to distribute the empty wagons on the various sidings running among the quarry buildings, and then finally to pick up the loaded ones and put the brake van at the end of them. Going down the hill Owen had plenty of opportunity to practise handling the brake, but still it was more by luck than good judgment that they stopped within reach of the water crane.

After that the day went by uneventfully. They went

81

on down to the coast, then made another trip up to the quarries to bring the men back in the early afternoon. Finally they collected the ordinary goods traffic bound for the coast, and after another trip to Port Elwyn and back, shunting at every station on the way, the day's work was done.

'Well, that wasn't so bad,' said Angus as they prepared to go home. 'You might have done much worse. Let me know what your brother-in-law says about being knocked over this morning !'

As they were walking away Mr Parker came out and called them across to his office. Heavens, that's torn it, thought Owen as they followed him. He must have heard about this morning.

'I'll see you first, Duncan,' said Mr Parker. 'Come in.'

Owen sat down outside and waited, with his head in his hands. What a long time they are in there, he said to himself; Mr Parker must be very angry. I wonder what's going to happen—will he give me the sack ? What could I do then ? I suppose I'd have to go back to the farm —the North Western wouldn't have me if I'd been dismissed from here, not with a bad reference. I suppose I'd have to go away, and get a job on some English railway —at Manchester, perhaps, or even London. What a terrible thing that would be.

Then the door opened and Angus emerged, smiling broadly. 'You're next,' he said. 'Go in.' Owen looked at him wonderingly. What on earth was he laughing at ? Surely you don't laugh when you've been dismissed ?

'Go on in,' said Angus again. 'It's all right.'

Owen walked in, not knowing quite what to expect.

'You know we have only two drivers,' began Mr Parker.

'Yes, sir.'

'I've come to the conclusion that that isn't really

82

enough,' he went on. 'One of them might fall ill, for instance.'

Owen nodded, plucking up a little courage. He didn't seem to be angry at all.

'So I think you should be trained to drive in case this happens. I've just asked Duncan what he thinks, since he's in a better position to know if you're suitable than I am. He seems to think that you've got it in you to make a driver, and is willing to instruct you. Are you willing?'

Owen said he was.

'Good,' Mr Parker said, and then proceeded to talk at some length on the attitude with which such a responsibility should be approached. Finally he brought up another subject. 'As a passed fireman, you will of course be paid somewhat more,' he said. 'So in a month's time, if all goes well, your wages will be increased to thirty shillings a week.'

With that the interview was at an end, and Owen started for home. He had managed to keep a straight face while he was listening to Mr Parker, but he could no longer restrain himself now, and when he met Angus, who was waiting for him down the road, they both burst into laughter.

'Well, what happened in the holy of holies, lad?' asked Angus when he'd got his breath back. 'I saw you outside looking as if you'd seen a ghost, sitting there with your knees knocking.'

Owen told him what had happened.

'So you're getting your raise in a month, are you? I suppose he's holding it back until he's sure you won't go piling the workmen up on top of each other!'

However, there were no more incidents, and Owen's instruction went smoothly. At the end of the month he was officially promoted to 'Passed Fireman' and received his extra pay. Not long afterwards the last Crewe man returned to the London and North Western, so Owen was promoted again, to driver. A new man was taken on to replace him, and worked with Angus; Owen and Robert, driver and fireman, worked on the other shift. Owen had achieved yet another part of his ambition.

## II

FOR the whole of the next forty years the quarries were the most important thing in the valley, and most people had a job connected with them in some way. And hand in hand with the quarry was the railway. It carried the men up to the faces and chambers and cutting sheds and waste tips in the morning and back again at night; it carried the slate away to the sea. It carried the quarrymen's wives on their shopping expeditions, and their children to school. It played some part in everybody's life. After a while, when the newness had worn off and the novelty had gone, people started to grumble and make jokes about it; its charges were too high, or the trains were slow, or late, or uncomfortable. But it was a good-natured kind of raillery, for it was difficult to be really angry when you very likely knew somebody who worked on the line ; and if a train did happen to be half an hour behind time you could always get some convincing explanation of it the same evening when the driver, or the guard, or someone else who knew, came home. So little *Jennie*, rumbling up and down the valley with the passenger train, became a familiar sight, and as well known to everybody almost as a member of the family. Sometimes she pulled the goods.

Owen was still lodging in the village, and went home only at weekends. It would not have surprised anybody who knew him to be told that he was going to spend the whole of his working-life on the railway, for he hardly ever seemed to talk about anything else. Once every summer he would ask for a week off, and would take the money he had saved and go travelling around the country on his own. He said very little about his holidays, beyond vaguely mentioning where he had been ; but from what he did say it appeared that his main object was to see as much as he could of railways operating in other parts of the country, and he was never so happy as when he was wandering round some big engine-shed in Leeds or Cardiff or Carlisle, keeping out of the sight of the Inspectors and Foremen, but learning as much as he could, making friends with the other engine crews and going out with them on their locomotives, and seeing how other people tackled the same problems which he had found. For there was not a great deal of difference, he discovered, between hauling fifty or a hundred empty slate wagons up to the quarries at Abergwernal, and hauling a coal train over the Pennines, or through the factory-crowded, slum-scattered wildernesses of the Midlands. There was still rain and wind and ice and snow to contend with ; the same suffocating tunnels and slippery rails. And coal smoke, and hot oil, and footplate dirt, and ringing steel were the same wherever railways ran and steam was king.

But Owen kept his stories to himself very largely because he couldn't find anybody who listened to them out of much more than politeness. It was not until he was in his twenties that this suddenly changed.

It began one windy day in November, when he was going off duty at midday. The rain had suddenly started to pelt down, and as he walked along the platform he decided that he would wait under the awning of the station building until it cleared a little. When he was under the shelter he stopped, wiped the water out of his eyes, and suddenly noticed a girl standing in the doorway out of the wind. She looked about his own age, or a little younger.

'Is the office closed, then?' he asked. 'I don't suppose they will open it now until the passenger train gets in in about an hour. What do you want?'

'Oh, I don't want to see anybody in the office,' the girl answered. 'I've brought Robert Hughes's dinner for him —he left it behind when he went out this morning.'

'He's on the train now,' said Owen. 'You won't want to wait here in the cold until he gets back. Give it to me, and I'll put it in the engine-shed where he'll find it.'

'Thank you very much,' she answered, giving him the parcel.

Owen took it, wrapped his coat round his shoulders, and sprinted off, head lowered, into the storm. A few minutes later he came splashing back.

'Are you Owen Roberts?' the girl asked, as he shook himself dry again.

'Yes, I am. How did you know?'

'Oh, Robert is always speaking of you as the driver he went to school with, and I knew he didn't mean that big Scotsman.'

'Oh, yes, Angus Duncan. No, I don't suppose you'd mistake him for me,' Owen answered. 'And who are you?'

'I'm Robert's cousin.'

'Ah, now I remember him saying something about relations coming visiting. You come from Chester, don't you?'

'Yes, but we haven't lived there long. This is the first time I've been here.'

'How do you like it?'

'It's very nice, although it seems to rain so much.'

'It's funny you should say that. I've been to several places in England, and they all said that about Wales. Yet it always seems to be raining there too.'

'Perhaps it does. Where have you been?'

'Oh, several places. I go each summer to see a different railway.'

The girl smiled, but she didn't laugh. 'That's an odd thing for a person to do who works on a railway himself,' she said. 'Don't you ever want to forget about your job sometimes?'

Owen thought for a moment. 'No, I don't think so,' he answered. 'It interests me, and I don't want to do anything on a holiday which doesn't interest me.'

'Well, perhaps I don't, either.' She paused for a moment and then said, 'I like your little railway here.'

Owen smiled a little wryly, and asked why.

'I don't know. You have nice little engines, which don't make so much noise and fuss as the big ones—it may be that. Or perhaps it's because the guard and the stationmaster are not such big, important people that they have no time to talk to anybody. Or maybe it's just because I've heard Robert talking about it so much I feel I know everybody who works here.'

'Well, you seemed to know me, anyhow.'

'Oh, yes, and I know all the engines' names, too. There's *Lady Gwyneth* and *Lady Margaret*, and there's *Jennie*, which Robert works on.'

88

'Well, you're quite right. How long have you been here?'

'Only three days.'

'You're doing very well, then. There are some men who have been here for three years who couldn't tell you the names of the engines, and women aren't supposed to be interested in them at all.'

'That's what Robert says, but he still talks to me about them, so I really have to be interested.'

'How much else has he told you about them, then?'

'Oh, he told me how they work, and how you make them go, and the names of some of the parts from a picture he had.'

'Did he, now?'

'Yes, indeed he did. But then, just when I had started to be interested, I asked him if I could have a trip on one of them, and he said I couldn't. He said it was no place for a girl.'

'Well, he's quite right, you know. You get very dirty, and there's a lot of noise and not much room.'

'Stuff and nonsense! I get dirty scrubbing the kitchen floor, but no man ever offers to do that for me!'

'Well, anyhow, you might get in the way,' said Owen, thinking of another line of argument.

'No, I can keep out of the way. Robert has told me what you do, and I can stand on one side.'

'And it's against the rules.'

'So Robert says, but he told me how you learnt to drive when only he was there, and that was against the rules, too!'

Owen laughed. 'Oh, so he told you about that, too, did he?' he said. 'He's been telling you a great deal too much! That's supposed to be secret.'

'Well, I won't tell anybody. But I don't think it's fair that you should break the rules yourselves, and then say to me that I can't come on the engine because it's not allowed.'

'Well, now, perhaps it is a bit hard. Robert and I are working together tomorrow on the goods train, and I'll tell him what I think of him then.'

'Yes, you do. And you can tell him that I won't stop pestering him until he lets me have a ride on an engine.'

'That will be hard for him,' Owen said, and then stopped. After all, what's the harm? he thought to himself. She looks a nice girl, too, and easy to talk to, not like all those other girls in the village who giggle and don't know one end of an engine from the other.

'What's your name?' he asked. 'Since you know mine, I'd like to know yours.'

'Elizabeth,' she answered. 'Elizabeth Hughes.'

'Well, listen, Elizabeth,' he said. 'If you really want to come, I can take you tomorrow afternoon, up to the quarries on the goods train.'

'Will you? That'll be wonderful!'

'Yes, but listen. You mustn't tell people about it, or we really will be in trouble. And you will have to wear overalls—you can borrow some from Robert, and tell him I told you so. You had better change into them here—there's a room in the engine-shed you can use. But we can't have anybody who looks like a girl on the engine, or Mr Parker will get to hear of it and there'll be a big row. So you can only come if you dress up as I say.'

He stopped; he had just come to his senses again, and realised what he was doing. But it was too late now.

'All right, I'll dress up, then,' Elizabeth was saying. 'I'm looking forward to telling Robert you said I could come, too!'

'I warn you, I don't suppose you'll enjoy it,' said Owen hurriedly.

'Oh, I will, don't worry! Thank you very much

indeed. I'll be here tomorrow. Look—the rain's stopped. I must go back now,' and she broke away and ran off.

' Mind you don't tell anybody,' Owen called out after her, but she was gone.

Now what on earth possessed me to say that she could come ? he wondered, as he turned back towards his lodgings. I shall get myself into trouble again over this if I'm not careful. And I know she will go telling everybody about it tonight ; the girl was never born who could keep her mouth shut. And I don't know what Robert will say.

Then he considered for a moment. Now what does it matter what Robert says ? he asked himself. I'm driver and I'm in charge, and it's not his business to object if I invite the whole of the Chapel Ladies' Guild into the cab. Let him worry if he wants to. And she seemed to be interested, and if she is, why shouldn't she come ?

Why not, indeed ? he was still thinking, as he washed very carefully behind his ears and brushed his hair unusually hard.

Next morning all went well. Robert arrived and said, ' She's coming all right—I couldn't stop her. What devil ever got into you to say she could come ? '

' I don't know myself,' answered Owen, but not as unhappily as he might have.

She was smuggled into the engine-shed while nobody was looking, and locked into the store room to change. It was fortunately a pay-day Saturday, and none of the workshop staff were on duty. Robert's spare pair of overalls fitted reasonably well, and when her hair was tucked up under her cap to keep the cinders and coaldust out of it, nobody just glancing into the cab would have realised she was a woman.

*Jennie* had already been prepared, so they had only to back down on to the line of empty trucks, couple on, and wait for departure time. With the three of them on the footplate it was a bit crowded when Robert wanted space in which to swing his shovel, but it was comfortable enough. Owen had padded the lid of the toolbox with a layer of cotton waste covered with paper, which Elizabeth said made quite a good cushion. 'I doubt if it will over the bumpy bits, though,' said Owen. 'If I were you, I should stand up when we start, otherwise you may bounce up and hit your head on the roof.'

The guard was also in the secret—he had to be. Fortunately, all he had said when he was told was, 'These young girls aren't what they were in my time,' and then appeared to forget about it. Now he leant out of his van and flicked a green flag, and they were off.

Owen was paying the most careful attention to his job. *Jennie* must not slip now; Robert had probably been telling her how careless it was to let an engine slip, and he didn't want her to think that he couldn't drive one properly. So while she watched him curiously, he opened the regulator as gently as he could, and very co-operatively *Jennie* made the smoothest start she was capable of. One by one the couplings clanged tight; finally the van curtseyed and started to move. Owen was looking back along the train; when he saw this he opened the regulator wider, and *Jennie* began to bark louder and gather speed. But he was looking back on the side away from the platform, Robert was firing, and Elizabeth was watching them both. So none of them noticed Mr Parker come running on to the platform as the train passed, and take a flying leap into the open door of the guard's van, clutching a brief-case.

The guard looked at him in horror for a moment. What on earth was the manager, of all people, doing on the goods train on a Saturday afternoon of all times? He always went fishing or something. This was awful.

'Are you all right, sir?' he asked, recovering himself. 'I hope you didn't hurt yourself, landing like that.'

'No, thanks, I'm all right,' Mr Parker answered. 'Glad I caught you—I have some unexpected business to do up in the quarries.'

'What a nuisance for you, coming so suddenly.'

'Yes, it is—spoilt my fishing.'

And not only that, either, the guard thought. While Mr Parker took some papers out of the brief-case and started to look through them, the guard considered what could be done. There was Elizabeth sitting in the cab ; if she was seen, there would be a very great row and no mistake. But how could he warn them on the engine that the manager was on the train ? It just wasn't possible. No, there was nothing for it but to sit tight and hope for the best. After all, most likely Mr Parker would go directly to the quarry offices and not anywhere near the engine at all. Then they might get away with it.

'Oh, by the way, is my scooter truck up at the top ?' Mr Parker asked. 'I may be some time, so I'll come down on it.'

'Yes, it is, sir—just opposite the office,' the guard answered. He was referring to a special truck, painted green and fitted with a handbrake, which was kept well oiled and used by officials who wanted to come down from the quarry in a hurry. If Mr Parker was going to use this, he wouldn't be about on the return trip, which was all to the good.

'It's Owen Roberts driving, isn't it ?' asked Mr Parker a few moments later.

'It is,' agreed the other, his heart beginning to sink.

'Good—I want a word with him. I'll go up to the engine when we get to the top.'

At that moment they went into the lower tunnel, so Mr Parker remained unaware that anything at all was wrong. He saw that the guard's face was green as they emerged from the tunnel, but *Jennie* was pulling hard and

93

burning a particularly sulphurous type of coal, so he attributed it to that.

Meanwhile on the footplate nobody knew what had happened. Owen was still trying to concentrate on his job, but *Jennie* was on her best behaviour, and he was not going to have much to worry about. He wondered how Elizabeth was enjoying her ride.

'How do you like it?' he asked her.

'Oh, it's fun!' she said. 'And it seems wonderful that you can make the engine do anything you like just by working those two levers. It looks so easy.'

'Easy? Well, she's going well today, but it's not always like this. Look out, here comes the first tunnel.'

Elizabeth moved back into the centre of the cab, and a moment later they vanished into the sooty cavern. Nothing could be seen at all except a thin red glare through the slit in the firedoor. After a moment *Jennie* struck a wet rail and began to slip, as she nearly always did. It would be easy enough to control her, but Owen was determined to put up a more exciting show than that. He let the wheels spin again and again. The noise was terrific; *Jennie* blasted a solid column of steam and sparks into the confined space, and in a moment it was hardly possible to breathe. It was like the Inferno. Owen continued until their speed had fallen quite enough. 'Let Robert think what he likes about this, so long as he doesn't say anything,' he said to himself. 'I'm going to give her a taste of everything.'

Their eyes were streaming when at last they emerged into the open air again, coughing, and gathered speed. Robert looked daggers at Owen, but kept quiet; Owen just grinned wickedly back, and then pointed out to Elizabeth how they were about to cross over the track on which they had been travelling a few moments before. They crossed the viaduct and swung into the upper tunnel.

This time Owen thought of a better plan, and in the dark he opened the sanders quietly. As a result *Jennie* never slipped at all, and since he shut them again as soon as the end of the tunnel appeared, nobody was any the wiser. Perhaps even Robert would think that it was all due to his consummately skilful handling of the regulator; but Owen doubted it. Anyhow, it would be quite good enough to deceive any non-railwayman, and it deceived Elizabeth.

'Well, that was much better,' she said. 'No slipping and much quieter.'

'Yes, I know,' said Owen, preening himself a little. 'I wasn't going to let her play up like that again.'

Elizabeth looked admiringly at him. 'You must be clever,' she said. Robert stifled a laugh, and pretended not to notice the angry look Owen shot at him.

After a few more minutes the quarry buildings appeared round the edge of the hill; Owen shut off steam, and they rolled gently to a standstill in the middle of the yard. Robert stepped down to uncouple the engine, and Owen started to explain to Elizabeth how the water gauge worked. The guard sat in his van holding his head in his hands, and Mr Parker walked up the length of the train and climbed into the cab.

For a moment there was a horrified silence as he gazed at Elizabeth, and then at Owen, and then back at Elizabeth. Then he recovered speech.

'Young lady, get off this locomotive,' he said. Elizabeth disappeared. 'Driver, what is the meaning of this out-rageous piece of indiscipline?'

Owen could only mumble and look at his feet. Then Robert climbed gaily back into the cab, but his whistle chilled on his lips as he met Mr Parker's gorgon glare, and he froze too.

'Your driver seems to have lost his tongue,' Mr Parker

said. 'Can you offer any explanation of this . . . this disgraceful escapade?'

'N-no, sir,' Robert muttered, and relapsed into silence also.

'Well, upon my soul, never in all my experience have I come across anything so shameful as this. With a reckless disregard for the safety of the train and of the company's property, not to mention the rules, you carry a passenger on the footplate—and not only a passenger, but a female! And you dress her up in your own clothes, hoping to impose deceit and avoid detection! I am absolutely appalled. I hardly know what to think of a woman who would consent to be a party to this escapade, and as for you——'

But this last was rather too much for Owen, and he was stung into speech. 'Sir—I will not listen to any slurs being cast on this lady,' he said, drawing himself up like a hero of contemporary melodrama. 'She came with her parents' consent, and at my invitation, and I am quite willing to take any responsibility.'

But this was hardly enough to abash Mr Parker. 'Indeed,' he said. 'I don't see that that improves the case in the slightest. Am I mistaken in believing,' he added, turning on Robert, 'that this lady is some relation of yours?'

'No, sir—I mean, yes, sir, she is,' said Robert.

'So.' Mr Parker considered a moment. 'Well, you deserve the most serious punishment for this, both of you. But I shall take into consideration the fact that this is the first time either of you have been in trouble. You will both be suspended for one week, and you may consider yourselves lucky to have escaped so lightly.' And with that he departed.

Robert and Owen looked at each other in silence for a moment.

96

'Where on earth did he come from?' they said together.

'What a nasty man,' said Elizabeth, climbing back into the cab. 'Was that Mr Parker? I hope I haven't got you into trouble!'

'You have, but don't worry about it,' said Owen. 'I asked you to come, and I'm glad you came. And anyhow he can't suspend us both because there isn't a spare engine crew.'

'Oh, good, I'm glad. But still I'm very sorry. You were quite right. I shouldn't have come.'

'Nonsense. Come again if you like, but when he isn't about next time.' Owen seemed to have cast discretion to the winds.

At that moment the guard came up and told them how Mr Parker had jumped aboard at the last minute, and how he hadn't been able to warn them. And then Owen told him what Mr Parker had said.

'Well, it could have been worse,' the guard said. 'But now we must be going, or we'll be holding up the passenger. He turned to Elizabeth. 'Perhaps you'd better come down in the van with me.'

'You can come down on the engine if you like,' put in Owen. 'He's gone away now, and won't know.'

'I'd better not,' she answered.

'Come on—I'd like you to.'

Elizabeth hesitated for a moment, and then made up her mind. 'All right, I'll come on the engine,' she said.

When they had finished shunting she came back on to the footplate. As they rolled gingerly over the start of the gradient, brakes grinding, she turned to Owen.

'I heard the whole thing,' she said. 'I was standing only just round the corner. I think it was splendid the way you stood up to him.'

Owen looked at her. 'Do you really think so?' he asked slowly. 'I felt pretty silly.'

'And did you mean it when you said I could come again?'

'Yes, of course I did. Any time you like.'

'Steady on!' said Robert. 'Mr Parker mustn't know.'

And Mr Parker never did. Or at any rate he never gave any indication of knowing about it, which came to the same thing. Elizabeth had several more outings on the engine, and as Owen had foreseen, neither he nor Robert were in the end suspended, although Mr Parker had more to say on the matter.

A week or so later Elizabeth went home, but from time to time Owen went to see her when he had a day off. During the following autumn, after nearly a year of writing laborious letters to her with pen and paper specially bought, and making the weary journey to Chester and back on Sundays, when nearly all transport was at a standstill, he proposed to her, and they were married a few months later. They went to Inverness for their honeymoon, because it was a long journey only to be undertaken on very special occasions, and the Highland Railway had a very interesting lot of locomotives. When they returned to Abergwernal and moved into their new home, the first thing they saw was a large flat parcel on the kitchen table, with a letter on top addressed in Mr Parker's writing:

'I am sorry this little present did not arrive in time to give it to you before you went away,' this read, 'but I understand that the photographer had some trouble with his enlarger. I hope you will like the picture, particularly as it is of the locomotive in whose cab I first met Mrs Roberts. I was sorry to have had to make such a disturbance on that occasion, but when a Railway Manager has a breach of the rules occur under his nose there is little else he can

98

do. On the other occasions I was fortunately able to turn a blind eye. With my best wishes to you both, Yours sincerely, William Parker.'

While Elizabeth had been reading the letter aloud Owen had been undoing the parcel, which proved to contain a large, framed, sepia-toned photograph of *Jennie*, specially posed on a part of the line with the lake and mountains in the distance, very scenic, and Angus scowling out of the cab at the camera.

' That's a very splendid photograph, isn't it ? ' Owen asked ; but Elizabeth didn't answer.

' The letter ! ' she said. ' Mr Parker must have known all the time ! '

' Eh ? My word, yes—I suppose he must have done ! '

They looked at each other in dismay for a moment, and then they both burst out laughing.

### III

THE next milestone in the history of the Gwernal Valley Railway was a few years later. By now there were four sets of locomotive men, as the railway was busy enough to need two engines in steam all day and every day. And although Owen was still only in his middle twenties, he had been a driver longer than anybody else except Angus, and was therefore senior to the other two. Now he usually worked the passenger trains, sharing the duty with Angus.

*Jennie* was very much the same as she had always been, and was still very sensitive to wet or greasy rails, and liable now and then to slip and misbehave. But Owen had become used to this, and had developed a sureness of touch and control, even more accurate and careful than Angus's, which always kept her moving, even when she was pulling the now much heavier workmen's train up to the quarries, with the early morning dew on the rails making the going difficult. He had come to know her so well that he could coax her into keeping time with loads that the other drivers could hardly have handled punctually with either of the two bigger engines. He had also taken over the responsi-bility for carrying out nearly all the minor repairs she needed, and so, since he could detect and cure every little defect as it began to develop, her complicated and special valve gear was still running as smoothly as it had done on Mr Pearson's test track. From time to time Mr Sullivan, who was still nominally in charge of the Locomotive Department, came up to examine the engines, and every time he came he said to Mr Parker how surprisingly well that 'patent plumb-crazy gear of Pearson's' was wearing. But then he went on to say glumly that it couldn't be expected to last.

One stormy night in November Owen and Robert were waiting at Port Elwyn with *Jennie* ready to work the ten o'clock passenger train, which now ran every Saturday evening to take the roysterers home when the pubs closed. It was a heavy train, as many of the quarrymen seemed to have come to the conclusion that the beer was better on the coast, and that a Saturday night at Port Elwyn was therefore a good thing. There were now four big bogie third-class coaches, as well as the luxurious first-class one with its stove and luggage compartment, and these were usually all packed so full that four or five of the little workmen's coaches, even though they had no lights, had sometimes to be pressed into service.

There was still fifteen minutes to go before departure time, and Owen and Robert were huddled in the cab, sheltering from the bitter sleety wind which whistled straight through from the sea.

'We'll maybe have a rough trip back tonight,' said Owen.

'What makes you think so?' asked Robert. 'We've had this load on a night like this before now and got away with it.'

'Oh, I don't know, really. But I thought today that she wasn't pulling as well as she should. There's something running a little roughly and she doesn't seem to handle quite the same. Nothing I can put my finger on, though. Haven't you noticed anything?'

'No, she seems just the same to me. You know, I think you spend too much time on this engine, crawling about underneath her and tightening things up. D'you know what Mr Sullivan said?'

'No.'

'When he was down here last he told Mr Parker that if you hadn't spent so much time on her, *Jennie* would have broken down long before this, and that sooner or later he wants to have her rebuilt with two cylinders like the other engines, so she'll give less trouble.'

'Why, what trouble does she give now?'

'Well, you know how he is—he's never liked her at all.'

There was silence for a few minutes, and then Owen said, 'It's strange, you know, that the other engines Mr Pearson built like this one haven't been any good at all, or so I've heard. He made a lot of them with three cylinders and valve gear like this one's, and they went out to places like South America and India. And they had such a lot of trouble with them that they've nearly all been scrapped or rebuilt now, and his firm got such a bad name that nobody would buy from them, and he's had to sell out and leave the business.'

'Has he, now? Well, I never thought that would happen to him. He looked as if he knew all there was to be known about engines when he was here.'

' So I thought, though he wasn't very good at driving them. Still, I expect the reason was that they didn't look after the engines very well in the countries they went to. If they were like this one, if only they'd treated them properly they'd never have had any trouble.'

' Well, Mr Sullivan said that, but he also said that no big railway would bother to take as much trouble with any engine as we do with this one.'

' Did he ? Well, that seems very wrong. Still, I shall be happier when we get back tonight. I think she seems to be spoiling for some kind of mischief.'

Departure time came and went, but that night they didn't get away punctually. For ten minutes after they were due out little knots of men came rolling merrily into the station, shouting that the train was to wait as there were more on the way. So it was nearly a quarter past ten before everybody was aboard ; the doors slammed shut against the pressure of people standing inside, and the guard swung his green lamp. *Jennie* laboured out of the station, turned her back to the sea and gathered speed towards the hills.

' She seems to be going all right to me,' said Robert, laying down his shovel.

' Yes, she seems better now,' agreed Owen. ' Strange, isn't it. I didn't like the way she was going this afternoon at all. Anyhow, we can try and make up a bit of time now. Elizabeth will be upset if I'm late.'

They stopped briefly at Castle Rock, and had already gained a minute or two when they restarted and began to climb through the woods. The long train wound slowly up the hill, the yellow lamplight from the coaches sending pale shadows dancing through the bare trees. Hafod Eithaf heard them coming from afar off ; *Jennie*'s labouring first of all, then the swelling noise of song from the train. Everyone in every coach was singing, and in each coach a different song was being sung. It made the night hideous, and by the light of the headlamp Owen saw a large tawny owl give him a long jaundiced look before spreading his wings and flying off clumsily into the darkness. A few of the passengers got off at Hafod Eithaf, but the noise was hardly any less as they drew on again, across the viaduct and out into the open on the long straight climb to the summit. They were still gaining time; in spite of the grade they were doing nearly twenty miles an hour.

Then, as they ran on to an embankment, *Jennie* seemed to falter for a moment, to hang back and then surge forward, while a new irregularity came in the exhaust. Owen grasped the regulator ready to close it, and leant out of the cab to try and hear where the defect was. Then suddenly hell was let loose. There was a great ringing, banging noise, and the cab shook violently. A fraction of a second later the whole of the front of the engine rose into the air, then with a great splintering, tearing crash fell sideways; and then, as the force of the moving train took hold of the back of the engine, *Jennie* slewed round, toppled over, and slithered down to the bottom of the embankment on her side. The first-class coach, which was immediately behind, took the full force of the blow, and one corner of the front end was stove in as it levered *Jennie* off the track and at the same time went down the other side of the bank. The rest of the train was brought up with a jolt, knocking down all the standing passengers, and derailing, but not much damaging, the second coach. This ploughed to a standstill, and then the couplings clanged tight as the other coaches rebounded and tried to roll back down the hill. A brief moment, and then a roaring of steam from *Jennie*'s safety valves, as the passengers slowly got up, rubbing their bruises and suddenly sober.

Owen had been leaning out of the cab when *Jennie* started to shake, and with the first movement he hit his head hard against the side of the cab. The second one flung him out of the cab and rolling down the embankment. He was already unconscious, but his hand was still on the regulator and pulled it shut as he fell. Robert felt the first shudder, and then the next thing he remembered was finding himself sitting half in, half out of the upturned cab, staring at his right arm, which looked strange. After a minute he realised it was broken.

The guard was sitting in his compartment at the end of the train, and was thrown to the floor by the sudden stop. However, he did not lose his wits. He knew that the rulebook said that his first duty was to go and lay detonators on the track behind, to prevent a following train colliding with them; but he also knew that there was no following train, and that there were more important things to be done. He got out and walked towards the engine. He didn't waste time asking if there was anybody hurt in the rear coaches, for if there was there would be more hurt at the front of the train and he would be needed there most. However, even in the second coach there did not seem to be any blood, and people were slowly climbing out. There was not anybody in the first coach, he knew; there had only been two first-class passengers, and they had both got out at Hafod Eithaf. So he did not look at it, but went straight on to the engine.

He first saw Owen, lying near the fence with blood oozing from a nasty-looking gash on his temple. But as he knelt down and started to loosen his collar he stirred and opened his eyes.

'That's a nasty cut you've got. How do you feel?' asked the guard.

'What happened?' asked Owen. He struggled and sat up, painfully. 'Good heavens!' he said, as he saw *Jennie* sprawling drunkenly, a shadow above the lurid light from her firegrate. 'Where's the fireman?'

'I'll go now and look for him,' said the guard. 'You just stay here and rest for a few minutes. You'll need a doctor to look at you.'

He went off and climbed round *Jennie*. As well as lying on her side, she was facing downhill ; her smokebox had smashed through the fence, and her front buffer beam had dug into the soil of the field beyond, while her cab was still half-way up the embankment.

The guard found Robert inside the cab, white with pain and with one arm lolling uselessly. In his other hand he held a shovel, and was struggling to remove the fire with it.

'You're in no state to do that,' said the guard. 'Leave it and sit down until the doctor comes.'

'Don't be a fool,' said Robert. 'She's dropped the plug.'

Even the guard knew what this meant, and was wondering what to do when he was thrust aside by Owen, who had followed him. 'Leave it to me, Robert,' he said. 'I'll get it out quicker than you can with that arm.' He turned to the guard. 'Help me lift him out.'

A moment later Robert was lying on the ground outside. The pain from his arm hit him like an axe as soon as he could forget about the fire, and his mind was so numbed he could scarcely realise what was going on. Owen had taken one look at *Jennie*, and realised that as she was lying, the water in the boiler must all have run forward, and that the firebox would be overheated. If it was not to explode the fire would have to be shovelled out in a matter of seconds. So he worked like a demon, and a shower of white-hot coal came shooting out of the cab door. The guard watched him for a moment before he realised that the passengers were shouting, and that there was a red glare coming from another direction. Then he remembered the stove in the first-class coach, and ran back towards it.

The stove had been well stoked up before the train left, and the shock of the accident had wrenched it from its fastenings and knocked it flying. The coals had shot everywhere; into the upholstering of the seats, along the floor and the walls, and the resulting blaze had won a good hold before anybody noticed it. Now the inside of the passenger compartment was an inferno, and the luggage compartment was well alight. Part of the roof had just fallen in, and the flames were roaring up into the sky. It was clear that nothing could now save Mr Pearson's masterpiece of coachbuilding, and that in fact prompt action would be needed to save the rest of the train.

The guard looked round for a second, and saw that about fifty people were grouped round in a half circle, waiting for him to move. He blessed the fact that he had forgotten to carry out another of the commandments of the rulebook, and did not screw down his brake before leaving the van. He had noticed that the coupling between the first and second coaches had broken, so that the whole train was only prevented from rolling downhill by the fact that the second coach was off the rails. He then saw what had to be done.

'Everybody get round the train and push it downhill!' he shouted. 'Quickly!'

In a moment everybody had found some hold, and pushed as hard as they could. The derailed coach moved, but only on its springs. 'Everybody together!' somebody shouted. 'One—two—three—heave!' The coach lifted again, lurched forward, and then ran on slowly, rocking and bouncing on the sleepers. The rest of the train was rolling freely and pulling it, and gaining speed; the guard rushed back alongside the empty coaches, then climbed aboard one and applied the handbrake. The cavalcade once more bumped to a standstill, twenty yards down the line now and quite safe.

And there it stayed until morning. The passengers began to straggle away and walk home ; after half an hour a doctor arrived, and set Robert's arm and gave him a sleeping draught. Owen submitted to his head being bandaged, but refused any other attention, and the doctor turned to treat some minor cuts and bruises that some of the passengers in the second coach had suffered. Word of the accident reached Abergwernal as the first passengers arrived on foot, and within a few minutes Mr Parker was out, had roused Angus, told him to raise steam and send a breakdown train, made arrangements to summon all the railwaymen living in the village to travel on it to the scene of the accident with all the necessary tools, and had borrowed a horse and was galloping towards Garthowen himself.

The clouds gathered once more, the wind rose and the sleet came down again, cutting into the flesh. The fires by the railway dwindled and vanished, and the red glare which had lit up the mountainsides shrank to a few smouldering angry sparks. *Jennie* still lay sloping down the embankment, her paint scorched and blackened, a gentle wreath of steam blowing up and away before the gale ; the first-class coach was nothing but a twisted steel frame, with a great waste of burnt timber and broken glass all round. The doctor had Robert carried to a nearby farmhouse, and Owen and the guard sat shivering in an empty coach waiting for the breakdown train.

## IV

THE breakdown crew laboured all the Sunday to clear the line and recover *Jennie*. The second coach was rerailed at once, and the train, including the remains of the first-class coach, was hauled down to Abergwernal. But *Jennie* was not so easy to deal with. Not only did she have to be hauled up the embankment and righted, but it was also found that one of the driving-wheel axles was broken. This meant that the driving wheels had to be taken out, and all the valve gear and coupling and connecting rods dismantled. Owen helped with this work until in the middle of the morning Mr Parker called him aside.

'Roberts, you've done enough now. You must go home and get that cut attended to properly.'

'It doesn't matter, sir—I can carry on for a while.'

'There's no need for you to—the others can finish. By the way, you know that there will have to be an enquiry into this accident, but Duncan tells me that it appears to have been caused by a breakage of some part of the locomotive. If that is true, you shouldn't have much to worry about.'

Owen paused. He felt that the accident was not his fault at all, and so therefore he should not have anything at all to worry about; but still, it was no use objecting yet. They would all find out soon enough. 'Well, I'm glad nobody was hurt, anyhow,' was all he said.

He went home and slept for eighteen hours. On the Sunday evening *Jennie* was slowly towed to Abergwernal supported only by her leading and trailing wheels, with timber blocks relieving the springs and preventing them moving sideways, and carefully pushed into the workshop, where she would clearly stay for some time. A wagon loaded with her dismantled parts followed her. The breakdown crew dispersed, the platelayers set about relaying the damaged track in time for the early morning train, and everybody in the village had a new topic of conversation which looked good for the next six months at least.

Owen and Robert were told they need not work for the next couple of days, and they were quite glad of a breathing-spell. Somehow, finding yourself lying on the ground with your locomotive upturned beside you is rather an unsettling experience. But the following afternoon Owen went with Angus to the workshops, and in company with the foreman fitter they both went fossicking among the broken pieces to see what had happened.

'Mr Parker said that he'd telegraphed to Mr Sullivan, and that he's coming up tomorrow,' said the fitter.

'Aye, to investigate the cause of the disaster, no doubt,' said Angus. 'Well, it seems clear to me what happened, and I doubt if he'll find any different. Look at the middle cylinder connecting rod,' he went on, indicating the tapered bar of greasy steel, with a grey, discoloured fracture at one end. 'That crack has been developing for some time, as you can see from the dirt that has worked its way in. And you couldn't have seen it, even if you were looking for it, since it would be hidden away behind the middle valve gear.'

'Yes, it would be, just there,' said the fitter with feeling. 'You could hardly get at the small end of that rod to oil it, let alone check the brasses. I've seen just the same thing happen time and again on the big engines.'

'But how did that bring us off the track?' asked Owen.

'Well, that's easy to explain,' said Angus. 'You were working her hard up the hill, I don't doubt, and probably going quite fast. When the rod broke, it whipped round once or twice, bending the valve gear about as you can see, and then it hit a sleeper and levered the engine on to its side. This must have broken the axle, too—although to go so easily that couldn't have been sound either. Anyhow, you can see the marks on the track of what happened —several sleepers were badly torn and split, and one was broken right in half and forced down hard into the ballast, just below where the engine was lying. And that spread the road and brought the coaches off as well.'

'It did more damage than that, too,' said the fitter. 'Did you notice the other thing it hit, not the valve gear?' He climbed down into the pit underneath the track on which *Jennie* was standing; Owen and Angus followed.

'There,' said the fitter, pointing to a great tear in the thin sheeting which covered the boiler lagging at the bottom of the barrel, a few inches from where it joined the firebox.

'Oh, aye, I saw that,' said Angus. 'The rod knocked a dent in the boiler sheeting, too.'

III

'Look again, and put your hand inside the tear,' said the fitter.

Angus reached up and did so. A little shower of powdered plaster from the lagging fell down as he drew his hand out and whistled softly. Owen felt inside as well.

'It must have hit here pretty hard,' he said.

'Yes, indeed,' said the fitter. 'You can feel how it has torn a great bite of steel out of the boiler plate itself. You were very lucky it didn't go right through.'

'We were,' said Owen. 'How can this be repaired?'

'Oh, I expect we could put a patch on,' said the fitter, 'but it wouldn't make a proper job. Besides, the firebox is very badly scorched and distorted, so they may decide to have a new boiler instead.'

'Well, well, all this is going to cost the company a pretty penny,' said Angus. 'One new coach and one new boiler. Still, don't worry about it, Owen, they can't blame you.'

'No, indeed,' said the fitter. 'Act of God, that's what it was.'

'And they must have known what a risk they were running having a stove in that coach,' said Angus. 'Mr Pearson may have got the idea from America, but I've heard that they have a lot of fires in trains over there for the same reason, so it's a pity he didn't think of some better idea to keep the first class warm.'

Owen climbed out, following the others. He was a little shaken by finding out just how much damage had been done. When Angus turned to leave the workshops he followed and caught up with him.

'Look, tell me seriously,' he said. 'Do you think they will blame me for the accident?'

Angus started to smile, but looked at Owen and thought better of it. 'Now listen, lad,' he said. 'Do you think you were to blame in any way?'

'Well, no—I don't see what I could have done.'

'All right, then. If you did everything you could reasonably be expected to do, you have nothing to worry about. As the fitter said, you wouldn't have been able to see the tiny crack in the rod before, and nobody can blame you for not seeing it. What the rod did when it broke is nobody's fault.'

'You really think that?'

'Of course.'

'Well, I'm very glad. Thank you very much.'

Next morning, when Mr Sullivan arrived, he examined *Jennie* and came to much the same conclusions that Angus had. A week later Colonel Richards came back to Abergwernal to hold an official enquiry, which involved taking evidence from everybody concerned, and inspecting the site of the accident, and taking measurements and making drawings of all the broken parts and of the engine and coaches as they had come to rest. Eventually he made a report, which was printed, and his conclusions were again the same. If anybody was to blame for the accident, he said, it was the man who designed the locomotive in the first place. Mr Pearson heard of this and exploded with wrath, but he could not do anything about it.

Meanwhile Mr Sullivan made another report to a special meeting of the directors. He described what had happened, and then went on:

'The effect of all this is that *Jennie* is going to be out of service for some time, and will in any case cost a great deal to repair. You have already agreed, gentlemen, to purchase a new first-class coach to replace the one that was destroyed. What I now propose is that the railway purchase a new locomotive. The traffic has risen to the point at which three locomotives could barely handle it, and it is still increasing. I think you will agree that *Jennie* was in any case too small to cope with her share of the work. At the moment there are only two locomotives serviceable, and so we must act quickly. Therefore I suggest that a new locomotive is ordered at once, and that in the meantime *Jennie* is left alone until we can decide what is to be done with her.'

After a discussion the directors agreed to this; for the railway was making quite a lot of money and could, in the circumstances, afford a new engine. After the decision had been taken, one of the directors raised another subject.

'Now what about the people who were responsible for the damage?' he asked. 'What action has been taken against them?'

Mr Sullivan looked up quickly. 'Nobody was responsible for the accident, and nobody was responsible for the damage,' he said.

'Come now,' said the director. 'I've never yet heard of an accident which wasn't somebody's fault. Whose fault was this one?'

'I think we have been into this before,' started the Chairman, but Mr Sullivan was already speaking.

'My dear sir,' he said. 'The official report of the Board of Trade Inspector, with which I am in entire agreement, is quite explicit on this point. The accident was not caused or aggravated by anybody failing to carry out his duties. If you dismiss the engine crew, as I understand you to suggest, you will not only be treating them unjustly, but will also be harming the company directly. For those men have had a valuable experience, since having suffered from one accident you may be sure that they will take good and special care never to be involved in another. And so they are more valuable to us.'

'Nonsense,' muttered the director who had brought the subject up, but the logic behind what Mr Sullivan had said was clear to everybody else, and the proposal to dismiss Owen and Robert died a natural death.

For the next four months Mr Parker was on tenterhooks in case there should be another breakdown, since now both *Lady Gwyneth* and *Lady Margaret* were working every day, and if either failed the railway would be partly paralysed. Fortunately nothing went wrong, and at the end of the four months the new locomotive arrived. It was rather like the other two, but a little bigger and heavier, and a very handsome machine. Mr Parker, as an Englishman, had been hard pressed to suggest a name for it which would be acceptable to the Welsh, and had done some diligent thumbing through the history books before coming up with a suggestion which he put before the Board.

'Concerning the matter of a name for the new locomotive,' he had said, 'I think it would be a good idea to name it after some historical figure who lived in the district, and I'd like to put forward the last sovereign and independent Prince of Wales, Owain Glyndyfrdwy.'

'Owing Glenwhat?' asked one of the directors, who was rather deaf.

'Shakespeare called him Owen Glendower,' explained Mr Parker.

Unfortunately the Chairman was a man of noble birth, who traced his ancestry back to the Plantagenets, and he scarcely liked the idea of naming one of the company's engines after a man whose head had been placed, he thought, on a spike by one of his kingly forebears.

'Not that rebel rogue,' he said. 'I think that would be most undesirable. On the other hand, I think your main idea is a good one. If we must rule out the last Prince of Wales, what about the first one?'

Mr Parker hastily riffled through the pages of his history book. 'A very good idea, sir,' he said. 'Ah, yes, here we are—Rhodri Mawr, or Roderick the Great, who was proclaimed ruler of most of Wales in 844.'

'Yes, I think he would do very well,' said the Chairman. 'Any objections?'

There were none, and so when the new engine had been lowered on to the Gwernal Valley tracks at Port Elwyn two large brass nameplates were bolted on to her tank sides, and *Rhodri Mawr* she became. It wasn't until later that Mr Parker remembered that the Chairman's name was also Roderick; but he kept his thoughts to himself.

*Rhodri* was towed up to Abergwernal, inspected, steamed for the first time, and gently run in as the others had been before her. Angus handled her, and said that she seemed very promising. Meanwhile, *Jennie* still sat on trestles at the back of the workshop, rusting in neglect.

The night before *Rhodri* was to go into regular service Owen was again driving the last train of the day up from the coast with *Lady Margaret*. They passed the scene of the accident, but a few yards farther on, just as the crest of the hill came in sight, there was a sudden bang and a roaring of escaping steam. No, not again! thought Owen, as he listened, but after a moment he realised what the trouble was.

'Burst steampipe,' he shouted to Robert. 'Keep the blower hard on and don't open the firedoor while the regulator's open, in case it blows the fire into the cab. We'll make it to Abergwernal all right.'

And so they did, crawling over the top of the hill, and coasting down to the village normally, although by then the fire had all been blown out through the grate and on to the track. There was no steam left when they arrived, but Angus was still there and *Rhodri* had enough to shunt the train away and put *Lady Margaret* in the repair shop behind *Jennie*.

'Well, that's her out of the way for a week or two,' said Owen, as they climbed out of the cab. 'And not my fault this time, either.'

'Nice considerate beasts, aren't they?' said Robert, referring to railway engines in general. 'If she had to burst a steampipe on us, she could hardly have chosen a better time to do it.'

Which was true enough, for once.

## V

By the end of the winter nearly all the damage caused by
the accident had been repaired. The first-class coach had
been rebuilt, on the old frame, almost exactly the same as
it had been before, except, of course, that there was no
stove. Instead, steam pipes fed from the engine, and
radiators, had been fitted to all the coaches, and since so
much plumbing was being done in any case, the directors
decided that they might as well at the same time fit auto-
matic vacuum brakes to the coaches, and this was done
too. Which meant that trying to stop a heavy train going
downhill on a wet day was no longer sometimes the kind
of thing that gave engine-drivers grey hairs. But when

the directors heard how much it would cost to put *Jennie* back into service, they winced, took a look at the depleted treasury, and voted to get along without her for the time being. So she was painted, greased, and sheeted over, moved still farther into one corner of the workshop, and left to brood in silence on her misdemeanours for seventeen years. In the meantime Owen and Elizabeth had four children (two of each kind), Angus and Mr Sullivan retired and were no more seen, Queen Victoria died, and in spite of all these things life on the whole went on very much as it had done before. The amount of slate the railway carried was still increasing, but slowly now; and three big locomotives could handle the traffic just as well as two big ones and one little one had done.

It was Mr Parker who set off the next development, at a Board Meeting just after the turn of the century.

'One thing I have noticed from the traffic this summer,' he said, during the annual discussion of the railways operating results, 'is the constantly increasing number of purely holidaymaking passengers who travel on the line. During the summer we frequently had to add one, or even two, coaches to the trains to accommodate these people, who usually seem only to want to travel up to Abergwernal, walk down to the lake, and travel back again—and we made quite a lot of money out of them. Some of the other narrow-gauge lines, as you know, are going after this traffic with considerable success. In my own view, we could do just as well as they have done if we tried. If we had some coloured posters put up at towns along the coast we could attract even more people.'

There was general agreement with this, so Mr Parker went on: 'I also think it would be worth while, as an experiment at any rate, to run passenger trains up to the quarries in summer. It is quite an impressive part of the line, and there is a very fine view from the top which I think people might be willing to pay to see. And since the majority of the tourists seem to travel back by the train they came on, we might as well not worry about the fact that there is no town or village at that end of the line, and have no scruples about taking the extra sixpence for carrying them to nowhere in particular.'

The other directors were rather surprised at what Mr Parker told them of the curious behaviour of tourists, but after some argument he had his way, and it was agreed that two passenger trains should be run every day during the summer season right through to the quarry yard, and a sum of money was voted to pay for an advertising campaign to attract the holidaymakers. The Board of Trade had to give permission for this, of course, because that part of the line had not originally been inspected and passed for passengers (workmen, of course, did not count). However, as the extension had been built to the same standards as the rest of the line, and was also signalled, this was only a formality.

And so during the following summer, for the first time, passengers were carried beyond the village and up the mountain, half choked in tunnels and bewildered by the windings of the train. The coloured poster which Mr Parker had commissioned was displayed in every town for miles ; it was a gaudy and unlikely scene to the technically minded, as it showed an improbable train, dragged by a locomotive which bore little resemblance to any the company possessed apart from the name, chasing its own tail in and out of a tunnel against a backdrop of lakes, crags, rocks and mountain sheep. But it performed its function admirably, and people saw it and came in droves to Port Elwyn for the ride. For some weeks there were so many that all the passenger coaches were not enough, and all the workmen's coaches had to be added too (Mr Parker, conscience-stricken, had some fourth-class tickets specially printed to be sold cheaply to the unfortunates who travelled in them), and two engines were needed to handle the load. This resulted in considerable dislocation of the regular timetable, since the slate traffic had to be worked by special trains during the night. It was the busiest time the railway had ever known ; the staff worked long hours, and Owen's eldest son Rhodri was hurriedly promoted to driver. The financial results were extremely satisfactory, and the directors were very pleased indeed.

'Finally, it seems likely from Mr Parker's report,' said the Chairman when the Board were discussing the news, 'that we can expect a flood of traffic at least as great next year. As you have heard, the resources of the railway were strained to the utmost to handle the traffic that developed this year. Mr Parker believes that we shall certainly need some new coaches and another locomotive. I very much doubt whether we can yet afford a completely new locomotive, so perhaps we should first of all discuss whether or not to repair that machine which has been laid up in the works for so long.'

There was a long argument about this, but it was the Treasurer who, as so often, had the last word. 'We have money in hand sufficient for two new coaches,' he said, 'but after that there is certainly not enough for another locomotive, nor even a very considerable rebuilding of *Jennie*. Would it not be possible to overhaul the machine ourselves and get it back into service as cheaply as possible ?'

It was agreed to enquire into this possibility, and eventually it was decided on. Two new coaches and the necessary new parts for *Jennie* were ordered. Mr Parker and the foreman fitter gave a great deal of thought as to how it would be possible to organise the repair, which would be the biggest job that had ever been done in the works. These had been intended only for routine maintenance, and laid out accordingly ; and the staff was quite small.

Apart from the foreman, there were four general fitters, two blacksmiths, a carpenter and two apprentices, and none of them had been with the railway long enough to remember the days when *Jennie* was running. In fact, since Robert had left some years before to seek his fortune on some new railway in South America, Owen was the only person on the mechanical side who had had any experience of *Jennie* and her awkward ways.

So he was taken off the footplate, and that winter he was put to work in the shops, to help the works staff to reassemble her. It took them more than six months. A temporary timber gantry had to be built in the yard, to lower the engine on to the new sets of driving-wheels, and to lift the old boiler out of the frames and lower the new one on to them. Then the new boiler had to be tested and inspected by the insurance company. This involved pumping it full of water at a pressure half as high again as would ever be used normally, to give a good safety margin, and a careful examination of all seams and stays. The reason why water was used instead of steam was precautionary ; for if a fault did exist, it would be revealed only by a harmless trickle of water and not by an explosion which would destroy everything and probably bring down the building as well. When the boiler had been inspected and passed, it had to be covered up with plaster lagging, and then bound up with the thin lagging plates which you see from the outside. Then came the biggest job of all : removing the three old cylinders and replacing them with two new ones, which were slightly bigger so that they would develop the same amount of power, and assembling and testing the new valve gear and coupling and connecting rods. These were made in the works, copying the gear fitted to *Lady Margaret* ; Owen was glad to see that this meant that the new parts were very much heavier and stronger than the ones they replaced.

Then finally came the job of fitting the tanks and cab and bunker on again, and all the steam, water, oil and sand pipes and fifty other small things.

Finally, as spring was turning into summer, *Jennie* was ready to take the road again. But she was no longer the same. The old *Jennie* had been a dainty machine, perhaps, but not really substantial enough for the work she had to do. The new *Jennie* was much less of a drawing-room ornament, but looked more convincing as a source of power. The new boiler was rather larger than the old one; and so she had to have a new, shorter chimney; and these two changes made her appear altogether more of a product of the twentieth century than any of the others. The old copper-capped chimney was replaced by a squat, unornamental stovepipe affair. The general effect was almost to convert her into an American plug-ugly, but perhaps there was not quite enough plumbing festooned over the boiler to make this impression complete. And she still had the same unmistakably English cab and bunker.

Owen took her out on her trial runs, and found that her behaviour had changed almost as much as her looks. She was not as fast as she had been; with only two cylinders she was not quite so well balanced at the front end, and with the larger boiler and higher centre of gravity she began to roll rather uncomfortably at about thirty miles an hour. However, she was quite fast enough for normal purposes. She still steamed freely, and seemed to burn slightly less coal; but the main change for the better was in her hill-climbing. The larger boiler and tanks had put more weight on her driving wheels, which was exactly what she had needed the whole time. There were no more of the thunderous, ineffective fits of slipping on wet rails; she settled down willingly to the long climbs. Owen tried some experiments to see how many coaches the different engines could haul up to the quarries on a wet day without losing time. *Rhodri Mawr* could manage eight; *Lady Margaret* and *Lady Gwyneth* could each take seven. In the old days *Jennie* had often had a struggle with four, but now she could deal with six without making any protests to speak of. And it was only in the busy part of the summer that the trains grew to more than six coaches.

All this was very satisfactory, for nobody had expected that *Jennie*, cheaply repaired with limited equipment, would be anything more than a stopgap to be brought out only when absolutely necessary. So the plans were changed, and she was put back on to her old duty of working the passenger trains the whole year round. When the busy season came, and once again it was found that in spite of having two new coaches, it was still necessary to hitch the workmen's four-wheelers on the back, *Jennie* was used to assist *Lady Gwyneth* or *Lady Margaret* on these trains, while *Rhodri* worked the goods. The next year two more coaches were built, and four a year later; and afterwards, almost every day for about six weeks every summer, an enormous train of fourteen coaches, with two engines (usually *Jennie* and *Rhodri*) used to blast its way up to the quarry yard in the mid-afternoon, laden with holiday-makers, crawling round the dizzy curves and across the bare, rocky screes, filling the valley with noise and leaving a pall of smoke hanging in the still air.

It was the railway's high-water mark, in those years before the First World War, and its prosperity was reflected in the dividends it paid. Unlike those who invested in most of the other narrow-gauge lines, the Gwernal Valley shareholders could not complain that they never had their money back. Their original investment was repaid more than twice; and in spite of this the railway was improved several times in those years. More rolling stock of all kinds was built; much of the track was relaid with new and heavier rail, and several sharp curves in the woods below

Hafod Eithaf were cut out when the line was deviated for half a mile on a straighter course, with two new ferro-concrete bridges over the river.

In 1912 Mr Parker retired, and in 1913 the slate traffic reached the highest level it ever attained. From then on it diminished ; slowly for the first decade, and then faster each year. The number of tourists continued to rise pretty regularly, except during the war, until the early 1930s ; but the local passenger traffic began to fall away to vanishing-point after buses started to run up the valley. And this meant that the line's whole character began to change. No longer was it an essential part of the way of life of the valley people, for its importance to them lessened year by year, and their old memories of it faded. The tourists came in their hordes ; but they knew nothing of the past. Only the railwaymen remembered.

# PART THREE

I

For some years after the end of the First World War the railway was only a little less busy than it had been. There was still a lot of slate coming down ; usually three trips a day were needed to handle it. But it had often needed four in the old days, and five now and then. And there were still four and sometimes five passenger trains each day in each direction, with more in the summer. So there were at least two locomotives in steam each day the whole year round, and four engine crews employed every day.

Owen was now almost sixty, but hardly looked it. His hair was turning grey, but his eyes were clear and his hand was steady. He had been transferred once again from the footplate to the workshops during the war, when the foreman fitter left. The company had done this only as a temporary expedient, considering that some forty years spent driving and firing locomotives would not have qualified him very well to take charge of the shops, and they only gave him the job because men were so scarce at the time that nobody with any better qualifications could be found. But they underestimated their man. Owen had never forgotten what Angus used to say about the value of education and experience, and he had never allowed his mind to go rusty. In fact, with the exception of the headmaster of the school, he was very likely the best-read man in the valley ; and by travelling so much round the country he had kept his knowledge of railway operation and technique up to date and well beyond what he needed in his job. Elizabeth had occasionally in the past tried to encourage him to leave the Gwernal Valley and go on to one of the main-line railways, where without doubt he could have done much better for himself. 'But why should I ?' he always answered. 'I've got all I want here —a good home, enough money, a job which always keeps me interested—and we're respected people here. Why should I throw all this up and go and live in some ugly, unfriendly city simply for a few pounds a month more ?' And as she grew older, too, she saw his point and never raised the matter again.

She was angry when Owen was promoted to the job of Works Foreman at a wage which, although it was more than he had been getting before, was less than the previous foreman had received ; and she made the mistake of telling him so. It annoyed him. 'Don't think I don't realise what has happened !' he answered. 'But if the management don't think I can do the job so well as the man before me, it is useless to rail at them if they pay me accordingly. The only thing to do is to prove them wrong by doing the job better, and that is what I am going to do.'

And that was what he did. He reorganised the wagon repair shop, and by adopting new methods of work he managed, in a few months, to return to traffic nearly fifty slate trucks which had been made idle by a shortage of men to repair them. The three oldest coaches had been laid up because, one after the other, they had developed an alarming unsteadiness, the cause of which had baffled the previous foreman; Owen traced the trouble to wear of the bogie pivot which, producing a slackness in the movement of the bogie from side to side, allowed a vibration which at a certain speed amplified the movement of the springs. It was quite an obscure and complicated fault, traceable originally to a notion evolved in the fertile brain of the unfortunate and lamented Charles Pearson, and of course none of the other coaches suffered from it. But it was quite a feather in Owen's cap to have located and cured it. And so after a few months his pay was increased to be the same as his predecessor's; and a year later it was raised again.

Rhodri, their eldest child, had been born in 1884. A daughter had followed a year later, and was christened Jennie. Gwyneth had arrived in 1887, but her name had been chosen against protests from Elizabeth's parents, who took exception to their grandchildren being named after locomotives. Elizabeth was frightened that the argument would be renewed three years later, when their last child was born, but fortunately it was a boy, who was christened Edward after her father, and the lingering discord in the family was thereby removed. Both boys, when they left school, had gone to work on the railway. Rhodri started as his father's fireman, and was promoted to driver during the manpower crisis which followed the success of the first year's tourist season. Edward left school about the same time, and took Rhodri's place with his father.

131

Rhodri married in 1904. His first child, born the next year, was a boy, Hugh; but two years later arrived a daughter, who was promptly christened Margaret, completing the series which it had not been given Owen and Elizabeth to finish. Edward married in 1914, during the first days of the war, and a few weeks later both the boys enlisted in the army and went to France. Edward never came back.

After the war Rhodri returned to the railway, and took over *Jennie* and her work on the passenger train. After a few years his own son was old enough to come and fire for him. This made three generations of the family all working on the railway, and was the excuse for a splendid party. A few years later Hugh married in his turn and had a son, Gwilym; which assured the succession and set Owen calculating that before he retired there might be four generations at work on the line.

The first bus service to start running up the valley was operated by a man who owned a garage at Port Elwyn. He bought an army lorry, built a body on it, and put it on the road one spring with quite a blaze of publicity in the local newspaper and a positive rash of advertisements and timetables left on shop counters and nailed to telegraph poles. It was almost as bad as an election. But although the proprietor needed no lessons on the value of publicity, his experience of operating a bus service was non-existent. The bus itself was slow, noisy and uncomfortable, and although it broke down fairly seldom, when it did things were quite disorganised, as he had no replacement and had to try to borrow another one from a different firm some miles away. However, on the whole his vehicle stuttered not too erratically up and down the valley as often as the train did, and sometimes as quickly. None of the tourists used it during the summer, and the railway did very well that year on the passenger side; but when autumn came and the visitors went away there was a noticeable thinning of the ranks on the train.

That winter was an extremely hard one. There had been a lot more snow than usual, and then in early January a blizzard started one Saturday night. It snowed all day on Sunday, and there was a high wind as well, so that when the snow stopped early on Monday morning there were deep drifts in places. Fortunately, after the first, very early, snowfall, Owen had decided to fit a snowplough to one of the locomotives, and had had a rough temporary affair of timber and sheet steel mounted on *Rhodri Mawr*'s buffer beam. It would not have been able to deal with drifts more than a couple of feet deep, but he had ordered the engine out on the Sunday evening, and several trips up and down the line during the night kept it clear. It took four hours to get through to Port Elwyn the first time, as *Rhodri* had had to charge some of the blocked cuttings several times before forcing its way through. But all was well by the time the workmen's train, which on Monday mornings made a trip to Port Elwyn and back before going up to the quarries, was due ; and much to their surprise the quarrymen found themselves at work within a few minutes of the proper time, after a journey through snow sometimes up to the level of the carriage windows.

The bus, however, was not having quite such an easy time. It was so cold that the driver had anticipated having trouble starting the engine, and had arrived specially early. He lit the stove in the garage office, leaving the damper open so that within fifteen minutes the hotplate was glowing red. Meanwhile he had filled two buckets with water, and put them on the stove one after the other, so that when the first had started to boil the second was not too hot to hold his hand in. He took the second bucket and emptied it into the radiator, let it stand for a few minutes, and then drained it again. He had once read of how a man had cracked the cylinder block of a car in cold weather by pouring boiling water into the radiator ; and for all its shortcomings he was fond of his bus and did not like the idea of doing the same thing to it ; still less the idea of paying for the damage. When the radiator was empty again he took the other bucket and poured that in. He then tickled the carburettor, adjusted the spark and the choke, spat on his hands and grabbed the starting handle. Much to his surprise the engine started on the first swing, with a crashing backfire followed by the usual shattering roar as it drove up to full speed, setting the tools on the workbench a-clatter and making the bus dance on its springs, before he could get round to the dashboard and close the throttle. As the bedlam subsided the owner, who also acted as conductor, walked in, rubbing his hands.

'What ho, Charley boy,' he said. 'Glad to see you've managed to rouse the old girl this morning. She can be a devil on a morning like this, can't she ?'

'Good morning, Mr Williams,' answered the driver. 'Yes, she can. But they taught us how to get the better of these engines in the army. And it was colder than this in France sometimes.'

'Oh ? What did you used to do there ?'

'Hot water in the radiator, like I did this morning. Never fails.'

'Good, good. Well, it's nearly time to go—we'd better get ready.'

'I just want to fix chains on the wheels—we may need them in all this snow.'

The driver went to the toolbox mounted beside his seat, and drew out two great lengths of chain. These had been supplied with all the other equipment and spare parts when the bus had been bought at a sale of army surplus stocks a year before. They had, however, never been used. The driver dragged them round and laid them out in a straight line on the floor behind the rear wheels. Then he clambered up into his driving perch and cautiously backed on to them. He slid down and started to arrange one round the wheel. After a moment or two he stood up, muttered under his breath, and then called out, 'Mr Williams!'

'Yes?' came the reply, muffled, through the office door. 'Ready?'

'No, indeed! These wretched chains are too short—they don't meet by nearly a foot. Come and have a look.'

Mr Williams reluctantly left the stove and walked across. 'Well, that's torn it, hasn't it,' he said. 'What can we do about that, now?' He paused for a moment. 'I suppose you will need chains, won't you?' he asked.

'Oh, yes, definitely,' answered the driver. 'The roads will be very treacherous on a morning like this.'

They considered the problem for a moment or two. Then Mr Williams said, 'Well, we'll have to do something quickly—we're late already.'

'There's only one thing I can think of,' said the driver. 'I don't like it very much, but I can't think of anything else.'

'What's that?'

'We can bind the ends of the chain together with a length of wire. It won't be a proper job, but it should last until we can get some new ones.'

'Well, we'll have to do that,' said Mr Williams. 'I'll do one wheel and you can do the other. Let's find a pair of pliers.'

So with that uncraftsmanlike remark the two of them cut off some suitable lengths of wire and set to work. It was not a particularly easy job, since it involved them in lying on their backs underneath the bus to secure the chains on the inside of the wheels; and Mr Williams found it harder still because he had never had any mechanical experience, and working with pliers and a length of wire was just about as far as his abilities as a fitter went. Besides, he was increasingly worried about the time; as he had said, they were late already and growing later still. The driver had finished his wheel and was on his feet again while the proprietor was still on his back on the floor, wrestling in the gloom with a recalcitrant piece of wire with half-frozen fingers. So on the whole it is not surprising that he should have thought, 'Ah, well, that 'll hold it,' and crawled out into the light again with the chain really quite insecurely fastened on the inside.

'Ready?' asked the driver.

'Yes, let's get going.'

And so they chugged out into the road. The snow had ceased and the sky was fairly clear, with moon and stars shining between the few clouds which remained. It was just beginning to lighten in the east; it would be a fine, hard day. The whole landscape was covered in white; the only patches of different colour were where lighted windows shone yellow here and there, and in the distance on the mountains some of the cliffs and rocks poked above the snow, and some of the fir trees were only partly covered. There had been nothing else moving on the road, except for footprints which led in the direction of the station; and the bus left two neat furrows as it rolled cautiously along, clinking gently.

There were no passengers waiting at the stop this morning, and so they drove on past and turned up the valley road. The way ran level for several miles, winding among the marshy fields; then when they had crossed the railway at Castle Rock, they started to climb through the woods. For the road ran higher than the railway along here, clinging to the mountainside along the edge of the forest, leaving Hafod Eithaf on a side road, and after the first climb running fairly level until the railway rose out of the woods below as well. Then, approaching Garthowen, the road bent away again and climbed steeply for a quarter of a mile to cross the ridge at a higher point, leaving Garthowen on another side road. This final climb was the hardest part of the run, and the bus always had to take it in a protesting bottom gear. It could not be rushed because there was a sharp turn at the bottom.

They made the climb near Castle Rock fairly easily, and the driver had grown confident by the time they picked up their first passenger, a mile or so farther on. But they had a lot of trouble getting up the Garthowen hill. In spite of the chains the wheels began to slip and slide, and it was only after a long struggle that they reached the top, with a plume of steam coming out of the radiator vent. They went very carefully down the other side into Aber-gwernal, where they arrived just in time to turn round and start back.

There were quite a number of people waiting for the bus, for many of the villagers remembered a time a few years back when such a fall of snow had blocked the rail-way, and they imagined that the same thing must have happened again. Only a few had heard the workmen's train on its way through about an hour before and knew better. So some of the regular railway passengers seemed to have decided to give the bus a try. The result was that it was almost full when it set out from the village, and with the extra weight on the wheels they made the easy climb to Garthowen in good time.

All this time the chain on the right-hand wheel, which Mr Williams had fixed, was slowly working loose. There was no way of knowing this ; there was no tell-tale noise or anything. The driver had intended to have a look at the chains while they were waiting in the village, but there was no time and he forgot about it. It held until they had passed Garthowen, and then, when he first applied the brake to steady them down the steep descent, it finally parted. The wire on the inside of the wheel broke loose, and with a rattle the chain wound free and was left lying in the road. The outside wire, caught in the end of the chain, had been bent into a hook, and this pierced the tyre as it tore away. There was a frightening bang as the tube burst; the wheel went flat at once, and the bus lurched over and started to bump. Worst of all, with the surprise the driver lost his head and stood hard on the footbrake.

The result, on a steep, slippery road, was just what might have been expected. They went into a skid, veering over towards the left; and as the passengers screamed and the conductor shouted, the bus slithered faster and faster towards the bend at the foot of the hill. The driver pulled frantically on the handbrake and fought with the steering wheel, but it was no use at all. At the speed they were doing they would never get round the bend, he knew; they would tip over. The only chance was to steer towards a gap in the roadside wall which lay straight ahead, and this he did. So, as some of the passengers started to leap off, they jolted off the road, sending up a spray of snow to either side, and bounded through the gap and along the cart road which led down towards the railway.

The driver realised then that although his decision was perhaps the right one, it was still not going to avoid an accident. For the cart track fell steeper than ever, and there was no chance of stopping their mad rush with the brakes now. So he steered for the railway embankment, which rose steeply, but not too steeply, about a hundred feet ahead. By now about half the passengers and the conductor had jumped off or fallen out, and were lying scattered in the snow like rubbish off a runaway dustcart. The bus tore through the hedge at the side of the field, and crashed to a stop as the radiator dug itself into the embankment. The jerry-built wooden bodywork was wrenched forward, and the fuel pipe must have broken. There was a hissing and a white cloud of fumes for a few seconds, as petrol sprayed on to hot metal; then it touched the exhaust manifold, and in an instant the whole front end was alight. The driver had jumped clear at the last minute, and as the others straggled down the hill they stood in a circle and watched the bus convert itself into its own funeral pyre. Surprisingly enough, it seemed that nobody was much hurt; several people had had a shaking, but no worse, doubtless because the snow had softened their fall. But the bus was a write-off. It made a splendid bonfire.

'Can't you do anything with the fire extinguisher?' asked Mr Williams, a little indecisively.

'No, good heavens!' answered the driver. 'I couldn't have got near it once the fire started, even if I hadn't had to help with getting the people out.'

The owner muttered something under his breath and walked away.

'What's the matter with him?' asked somebody. 'It was insured, wasn't it?'

There was a pause, and then the driver answered, 'Yes, it was insured all right—but he had borrowed money to pay for it, and hasn't paid it all back yet. This is going to knock his business on the head.'

There was a murmur of sympathy from the crowd, but Mr Williams didn't hear it. He had reached the main road and seemed to be walking back home.

'Well, he may have the right idea,' said somebody else. 'We can't stand round watching this all day; some of us have a living to earn. What do we do now?'

'Walk home, too, I suppose,' said another passenger; but just at that moment there was a whistle and *Jennie* swept into sight coming down the hill with the passenger train. Rhodri, who was driving, saw the column of smoke rising from beside the line and braked, and they stopped just short of the blaze. Owen, who was aboard the train, leant out of the window and watched.

'Having trouble?' asked Rhodri.

'See for yourself,' answered the conductor.

Owen clambered down the embankment and took charge of the situation. The bus was well alight, but not burning now quite so fiercely as it had been; all the petrol had gone. On the other hand, the hedge was beginning to catch fire.

'We'll have to stop this spreading,' he called out to Rhodri. 'Can you bring the engine closer and spray the fire with the coal hose?' He turned to the crowd, and said, 'It'll help to put the fire out if you throw snow at it.' After a moment he added, 'If any of you are hurt, get into the train in the warm.'

For the next ten minutes all was bedlam, since the train was carrying about fifteen boys to the grammar school at Port Elwyn, and an invitation to throw snowballs was more than they could resist. By then the fire, although still burning, was beginning to look a little discouraged. So Owen ordered the train on, and bade them tell the fire brigade, while he remained behind with the driver to see that the flames did not spread again. Rhodri blew the whistle, the firefighters climbed aboard, and *Jennie* took the train, and the passengers who had deserted her as well as the ones who had remained faithful, on to the coast.

Some of the bus passengers offered to pay their fares, but the guard refused to take the money. 'This is on the house,' he said. 'In any case, we can claim from the bus company.'

'Ach, the dreadful smelly thing,' remarked an old woman who had deserted the train for the first time that morning. 'I was near frightened out of my wits when we started to slide and bounce down that hill. I'm not going on one of those noisy, rattling things again.'

'It's safer by rail, Ma, isn't it?' said someone sitting near by.

There was silence for a moment, then an old man in another seat asked the guard, 'Isn't that the same place where the train had an accident and one of the carriages was burned?'

'A good while back that was,' said another.

'Yes, that's the place,' said the guard. 'On that same embankment, and no more than a hundred yards farther down the hill. But it must be forty years ago that happened —I remember it, but it was before I went to school.'

'Ah, yes, it's a long time ago,' said the first old man. 'The little train's been running ever since then without an accident—and now this nasty new-fangled thing blows up and burns before it's been on the road twelve months.'

## II

THAT was the end of competition for that winter, and once again the people of the valley had to depend on the railway. In fact, they came to depend on it more than ever before or since.

Two days later the snow came again ; and if the first blizzard had been bad enough, it was only a taste of what followed. It snowed with scarcely a break for five days, and a howling wind lashing in from the sea piled the snow in drifts sometimes twenty feet deep. All Thursday an engine was out with the snowplough, in addition to the trains, but by the evening it was clear that the railway was fighting a losing battle. The last train up to Abergwernal on Thursday night stalled in a drift between Hafod Eithaf and Garthowen, and if it had not been for the fact that *Rhodri Mawr* was waiting in the loop at Hafod Eithaf and came to *Jennie*'s rescue within minutes, it would have been stuck there for a very long time. With both engines, the train finally rolled into Abergwernal nearly an hour late. *Rhodri* set off back to Port Elwyn with the plough at once, and got as far as Garthowen. But by then the big drift had become so deep that the engine could not penetrate it except by charging it at speed with the falling gradient to help, and clearing the way a few yards at a time. Success was in sight when, at the far end of the cutting, *Rhodri* was trapped and could not move either way. *Lady Gwyneth* was sent for, but by then more drifts had formed between Abergwernal and Garthowen, and these had to be cleared. At about three in the morning the engines met, and together managed to force their way down to Castle Rock ; from there to Port Elwyn there was less snow and no drifts to worry about on the flat ground. But they had to go to the end of the line for water, and during this half-hour's delay the cuttings behind them filled again and became quite impassable. The attempt was made, but the only result of it was that by Friday morning the two engines were stuck helpless in the big drift ; they ran out of water and their fires had to be dropped. And so traffic came to a standstill. *Lady Margaret*, during the small hours, had made an attack on the line going up to the quarries ; but by daybreak it had been decided to abandon the attempt to keep that part of the line open and to concentrate every effort on the main line. But now even this had proved impossible, and when the news arrived that *Rhodri Mawr* and *Lady Gwyneth* were marooned, and the snow was still falling, it was decided to give up the struggle and wait for the storm to blow itself out.

At that time the road was still open, since not so many drifts formed on its higher location along the hillside. But it became more and more difficult for anything on wheels to get through, and the last car which managed to complete the journey arrived in Abergwernal on Saturday evening. Early on Sunday the news came that there had been an immense avalanche from the overhanging mountain, blocking the road near Garthowen, which it would take several days at least to clear. And by then all the telephone lines were down. So Abergwernal resigned itself to a snow siege and complete isolation. There was little anxiety ; the village had stocks of food and fuel for a week. Things were not quite so good at Hafod Eithaf or Garthowen, but even there they were supplied for several days.

And so at first nothing was done. People sat around in their houses, keeping warm, and expressing varying degrees of thankfulness for yet another holiday so soon after Christmas. The snow stopped on Monday afternoon, but little effort was made to clear it. What was the point ? everybody asked. Snow never remained on the ground in any quantity in the lower parts of the valley for more than a day or so. Why make unnecessary and frantic efforts to get the road open when the thaw would come and open it for them even more quickly than they could clear it ? It was not till Wednesday dawned without any sign of a thaw that this attitude began to change ; and by then people were beginning to feel the pinch and reports were coming in that this snowfall was something much more than had been known before.

On the Wednesday morning the railwaymen started on the work of clearance once again. By the afternoon the rest of the villagers had decided that in view of the avalanche which blocked the road, it was going to be a lot quicker to get the railway running again ; and that as the thaw still showed no sign of coming, every able-bodied man should turn out and help to clear it. The sooner this was done the better, for coal supplies were now very low, and food was beginning to run short.

So the work was organised, with gangs of so many men on each section of line. *Lady Margaret* and *Jennie* were brought out to help. During the previous couple of days Owen had had a second makeshift snowplough rigged up and attached to *Lady Margaret*, and with the two engines pushing behind this, and thirty men with spades, shovels, buckets, and even one man with a big broom, to help in the deeper drifts, by Wednesday evening the line was clear from Abergwernal through Garthowen as far as the beginning of the deeply buried section where *Lady Gwyneth* and *Rhodri Mawr* were stuck. 'Entombed' might have been a better word, for the snow had drifted up all round them, and only their chimneys, domes, and cabs could be seen.

That morning, the man who ran the village chemist's and stationer's, who had recently boldly laid in a stock of photographic materials, had shut up shop, put on a pair of snow-shoes, strapped his enormous plate camera to his shoulders, and using the tripod as an alpenstock had set off to record the snow scenes for the benefit of posterity. During the afternoon he came across the two engines, and took the photograph which was later framed and hung in the manager's office for many years. On his way back he found the gangs at work clearing the line, and saw another opportunity. There were about two hundred people there, and he took photographs of men posing leaning on their shovels until he had used up all his plates. Since most of them later bought copies of the photographs, he at any rate did rather well out of the storm. In fact, there was still something left of his profits when he had bought a splendid and more portable new camera.

Work started again before dawn on Thursday, and now all the effort was concentrated on the long cuttings above Hafod Eithaf and the short, but very deep one on the deviation just below the station which had been built before the war. By the early afternoon the two stranded engines had been exhumed, and were dragged out of the cutting by the others. All four went up to Garthowen; then *Jennie* took the two down to the village to be thawed out and *Lady Margaret* returned to the fight. But the worst was over now. *Jennie* came back at half past four, as it was growing dark, and by then only the last cutting, just above Castle Rock station, was still blocked.

Rhodri and his son Hugh were working on *Lady Margaret*. When *Jennie* came slowly up behind to couple on once again, Rhodri called across to the leader of the clearing party.

'It's getting late, now,' he said, 'and you're all cold and tired. I think that with the two engines we may be able to charge this drift and go through—but if we can't make it you'll have to dig us out. How d'you feel about it—will you take the risk, or would you prefer to play safe and dig it out first?'

The other man thought for a moment. 'I think we should chance it,' he said. 'There's a lot of people without coal up there, and they'll have a chilly night of it if we don't get through. Let's try.'

Another man standing by, one of the platelayers, said, 'There's something else that you'll run the risk of, too. If you charge that cutting too hard, and it's on a sharpish curve, you'll throw the engine off the road, and we'd be here all night getting her back on.'

The leader looked enquiringly at Rhodri, who said, 'Yes, I know that—but I don't think it's much of a risk. It's not happened so far, anyhow, in the other cuttings we've charged.'

'Ah, yes, but they weren't curved so sharp,' said the third man.

'I think we'll be all right,' said Rhodri.

'Well, try it, anyhow,' said the leader. 'If you win, we've finished—if you don't, we'll not be here much longer than we would in any case.'

'Right,' answered Rhodri. 'Tell them to stand clear, then.'

He had a word with the other driver, and then the two engines backed up the hill a little way, whistled, and charged. They were doing nearly thirty miles an hour, regulators wide open, when they hit the snow and sent it flying in a fan-shaped spray high into the air. Rhodri felt *Lady Margaret* back and sway as she hit the drift, and for a moment as he lurched he felt that perhaps the platelayer's warning had been justified. But just at that instant *Jennie* stopped pushing, as he had arranged with her driver, and put her brakes on for a second. This sharp tug from behind just after they hit the snow pulled *Lady Margaret* back on to the straight again, and counteracted the tendency of the snow to pile up on one side of the plough and force her off the track. And so when *Jennie* started pushing again a moment later *Lady Margaret* was set square.

The question now was whether the two engines could keep moving. Their impetus had carried them half-way through the cutting, but now they were moving at a bare walking pace, their exhausts woolly and laboured as they slowly thrust the powdery, cloying snow to each side. For a moment, with twenty yards to go, it hung in the balance whether or not they would stall and have to be dug out. By now their speed had fallen further, and the men watched through the dusk and listened anxiously whether they were still moving. From time to time *Lady Margaret* would start to slip as the snow forced under the plough and started to take the weight off her wheels, but after a

147

moment it would roll clear and she would settle down again. Then suddenly she began to slip worse than before, and didn't recover ; perhaps it was ice on the rails, for a moment later *Jennie* started slipping as well. Then there was silence, and the men sighed and picked up their shovels to dig the engines out. But just as they started to move, first *Jennie* and then *Lady Margaret* started to work again. It was desperately slowly this time ; nearly a second between each explosive bellow from each engine, until *Lady Margaret* suddenly started blowing off and the roar from the safety valves drowned all other noise. But by now the cutting was becoming shallower, and after a minute the engines began to accelerate perceptibly. A minute later they were moving quite fast ; and then they stopped and whistled as a signal of victory. A cheer went up from the crowd, and they began to clamber aboard the wagons on which they had ridden from the village that morning. Then the two engines came thundering back through the cutting, *Jennie* scraping snow off the sheer sides and scattering the piles which had fallen back in after they had passed through.

Rhodri got down and spoke to the leader again. ' We'll have to go down to the coast now,' he said. ' There's a train there all loaded up with coal and food to be taken up tonight. So we can't take you all back home just yet. I'm going to take the wagons down to Castle Rock, and put them in the siding there—and we'll pick them up on the way back.'

So the workers climbed aboard and were taken down the line to Castle Rock. Realising that it might be some little time before the engines came back, one bright lad who was feeling the cold suggested lighting a bonfire on the platform. This seemed a good idea, so in a few minutes brushwood, dead leaves, branches and logs enough to make a sizeable Guy Fawkes Night blaze had been gathered from the woods and set alight. They had stacked it up against one side of the little station building out of the wind, to give the kindling flames a chance, and it was not until the fire was burning strongly and the first song was sung that anybody noticed that the hut was not stone, but wooden. By then it was too late to do anything about it, and when the train came there was very little left of station or bonfire. Naturally, there was quite a lot of argument about it all later. The company wanted to know who was going to pay for the damage, and the people living near the station wanted a new and more comfortable shelter. Nobody ever got any satisfaction, as it turned out ; the company never obtained redress, and what with one thing and another a new station building was never put up.

But there was no point in crying over spilt milk when the train returned. There was some delay while the fire was put out and the wagons put on to the rear of the train, and it was nearly nine before they all arrived back in Abergwernal. There was quite a crowd in the station yard ; mostly women, with buckets, handcarts, and one or two elderly prams, waiting to collect coal and food. They fell on the train almost before it stopped, and in a few minutes it was stripped bare. The butcher and grocer were there with barrows, and unloaded several sides of beef and sacks and boxes of provisions which they wheeled away quietly through the goods yard. One or two sharp-witted housewives, who had not ordered and paid for their coal in advance, thought that if they followed they might be able to avoid payment altogether ; but the village constable had read their minds and turned them back along the platform, where the manager, porter and booking clerk were busy with scales and till, weighing how much each person had taken and charging accordingly. However, everybody had what they needed, and each family was warm and well fed that night, in some cases for the first time for several days. It was a week before the great slip which had blocked the road was cleared, and during that time the village was supplied and kept in touch with the outer world only by means of the railway, as it had been until after the end of the war. But it was never to depend on it again.

### III

THE buses had been beaten back, but not for long. Before the summer Mr Williams sold his remaining assets to another firm which was already operating in the district, and the new owners lost no time in starting a service with better vehicles. The new buses were faster than the train, no less comfortable, and slightly cheaper. Although the railway company did what it could to compete, there was no getting round the fact that the buses were more convenient for most people. Several times a day they now ran through to Chester and the other towns along the coast, while the railway users always had to change trains at Port Elwyn. That winter the passenger train was cut down to one coach only, where three had always been needed before ; and the line lost so much money in running empty trains that the following winter the separate passenger service was given up, and the coach hitched on to the back of the goods train instead. The service was now slower, and ran much less often, but it was less ruinously expensive to put on. For the only people who used it now in the winter time were those few who happened to live much nearer a station than a bus stop.

But the company had never made very much money from winter passengers, and if there had been nothing else for it to worry about it would still have been fairly happy. But there were other clouds gathering. Some of the goods and parcels traffic for the village began to go by road, which meant further loss ; and worst of all was the slow but steady decline in the slate traffic. This was not due to road competition, as no lorry was ever able to climb the track which led to the quarries ; it was simply because slate was becoming less and less in demand over the whole country. Tiles began to be used for roofs, bricks or concrete or even corrugated iron for the buildings near by, and real marble or granite for gravestones, while the bottom suddenly dropped out of the market for writing-slates which had been used in schools and offices.

As a result of this both the railway and the quarry, now once again separately owned, began to get into money difficulties. The quarry company was worse off, as it had no other source of income at all. Year by year, as the orders fell away, it had to cut down the number of quarrymen, until by 1929 only one face in three was being worked. This had effects in the village ; houses became empty as people went away to try and find jobs elsewhere ; and on each street corner the men who could not bear to uproot their families and abandon their homes lounged about, talking dispiritedly, and hoping dimly that things would get better. The general atmosphere was much the same at the Board Meetings of the two companies.

The railway lost money for the first time in 1929, and the directors decided to make drastic economies. The number of platelayers was first halved, and then a few months later cut again ; so that the remaining men had their hands full in patching up and repairing the weak spots in the track. They were still able to keep it safe ; but grass began to grow between the rails in places, and the banks and hedgerows along the lineside ran wild, and after a few years were rotten with rabbit warrens. At the same time it was decided that with only one train on the line at a time for nine months of the year, signalmen were an extravagance. The signal boxes at Port Elwyn and Abergwernal were put in charge of the booking clerk (who was also the porter), and most of the signals were taken out at the same time. There had been no signalmen regularly employed at Hafod Eithaf or the quarry yard since the middle of the war, and now all the signalling equipment at these places was dismantled, and hand levers installed by the side of the line to work the points. Strictly speaking this should not have been done, and no doubt the Ministry of Transport would have had a few things to say about it ; but nobody thought to write to let them know. After a little while the few signals which were left began to be disregarded, and stood at ‘ clear ’ all the time. With only one train on the line and no possibility of collisions, the porter-clerk saw no point in leaving his nice warm office to go into a damp, musty signal box to ‘ pull off ’ for it. And so the signals were not bothered with except perhaps when things were busy, or when the General Manager came on a visit from London.

For that was another change ; keeping a manager employed on the line was considered extravagant now, too ; for there was very little left for him to do. Fortunately the old manager was on the point of retiring in 1929, so the directors were spared the embarrassment of sacking him ; they just gently helped him over the edge. He was presented with a clock with an engraved plate on it, and packed off to Bournemouth to die of boredom. Nearly all his functions were taken over by the company's solicitors, one of whom was appointed Manager just so that nobody could say there was no such person, and every two or three months he came down for a day to look things over and see to any business that needed settling on the spot.

But it was still necessary to have somebody in charge of the railway, even if only as a kind of foreman, and since Owen was now the obvious choice for this job, he got it. And he had time to spare for his new duties, since the amount of work done in the shops and sheds was less, and fewer men worked there. With less traffic, there was of course less wear and tear on the rolling stock, and so fewer repairs were needed ; and with less money some repairs were put off, or never done at all. If a wagon was in a bad way, it was easiest to put it on a siding behind the works and forget about it, while the brambles grew round and covered it up. There were plenty of other ones lying idle. And the locomotives had to wait longer for their routine overhauls. Owen did not like this, but he saw the necessity, and he had the gift of being able to judge exactly how long a repair job could be put off without making it worse. He grated his teeth as he heard *Rhodri Mawr* roll down the hill, with the rods clashing and ringing with the wear in the brasses, but he knew that however little he might like the noise it did not mean anything serious until it grew a little louder. The directors realised he had this ability, and knew that they could afford to cut their provision for maintenance while he was in charge of the works. Owen didn't see it quite that way, naturally, and grumbled at the risks he was having to run. But failures and breakdowns were few and far between; and it was very largely due to him that the extra economies were possible which kept the line from actually losing money again.

There were one or two other changes. It had been years since any slate had gone away from Port Elwyn by sea, and the harbour was silted up so that it could only be used by small boats; so the half-mile of track leading round the town, under the main line and on to the quay, was pulled up and sold for scrap. The train mileage during the winter months was cut again, and now the timetable showed only two trains, carrying both goods and passengers, each way every day. Now and then it might be necessary to run a third trip at midday to clear an accumulation of slate; but normally the only other train was the work-men's, which still made a trip to the coast and back every Monday morning to carry the few remaining quarrymen who lived at Port Elwyn and stayed in the barracks at the quarries all the week. During the summer there were still three or four passenger trains each way, and then perhaps three days a week another engine would have to be steamed to work down the slate which the passenger trains were too heavily laden to cope with.

Thus the railway pulled in its belt, and it began to look as if it would manage to weather the storm until, as many still hoped, the slate trade recovered. But five or six years went by without any sign of this happening. The village greybeards were never tired of repeating that the quarries were mere nibbles at a whole mountain of good, workable slate; and that there was enough there to keep everybody in a village twice the size of Abergwernal employed, full time and overtime, for five hundred years; that it was a scandal and an outrage, and all the fault of the quarry company, the county council, the government, the banks, or even sometimes the Americans. Nobody thought of blaming the people who decided they preferred tile roofs, although of course they were the real villains. Still less did anybody dare to point out that although many smaller quarries all over North Wales were closing, the biggest and oldest ones in Snowdonia seemed to be pretty busy still. This may have been because only the best slate could now sell, and the Abergwernal slate was not so good as the Snowdon ; in fact, this was probably the truth of the matter ; but it would have been rashly tactless for anyone to have said so in Abergwernal.

It was therefore no very great surprise to people who had been watching matters from outside, but a shock like a thunderbolt to the villagers, when eventually in 1936 the quarry company went bankrupt, and a bank took over. There was an uneasy pause after this disaster, and then dismay when the bank announced that it proposed to shut the quarries down. The directors of the railway held an urgent meeting to discuss things ; but before they were able to do anything the initiative was taken by the villagers. Abergwernal had been in uproar ; there was a public meeting at which many most magnificent speeches were made, emphasising the fact that the village was facing a sentence of death, and finally a protest march was organised. About forty quarrymen formed up in the village square, carrying banners which said *Save Our Homes* and *We Want Work—Not the Dole*, and similar slogans. And they marched all the way to London, singing (wherever there was a sufficient audience). When they arrived they went to the City, with crowds gazing and newsreel cameras grinding, and their leaders went into the bank to plead their cause. And as it happened, the bank relented slightly. They might have been going to reconsider the case anyhow, or they might have been touched because the quarrymen had marched to them first, and not to Parliament to demand that the Government should compel them to do something. But for whatever reason, it was agreed that the quarries should be kept open for a 'trial period', and the deputation returned to Abergwernal in triumph.

Then, for a while, it seemed as if better times had come at last. For the bank really tried to make the quarries a success once again. They put a great deal of effort into drumming up new business, and also spent several thousand pounds on new machinery. After a few months one of the abandoned working faces was reopened, and extra men taken on. This meant more traffic for the railway, and Owen had to have some of the wagons in the overgrown sidings hacked free, repaired, and put back into service. So although the years of stringency were beginning to leave their traces—some of the coaches and buildings began to look as if they needed new paint, the remaining signals had been taken away or fallen down, and the bushes by the lineside had started to rub against the trains as they went past—for a time there was new hope on the railway. At any rate, Owen consoled himself by thinking, we can handle the traffic still. All the engines are in working order, more or less, and although the Company has cut maintenance to the bone, it has cut it no further—it's still quite safe to do twenty-five or thirty miles an hour even if it is a little rough now.

And he would sometimes say to Elizabeth in the evening, that while so many other small independent railways in Wales and all over Britain were dying, being uprooted, and leaving nothing more than a swiftly healing but never-quite-obliterated scar on the land, and boys becoming men who could hardly remember the little trains which used to rattle through the green fields and along the riversides by their homes, it still looked as if this would never happen to their railway.

But in this Owen was deluding himself, for once.

## IV

At the beginning of 1939 it was clear that Owen's wish to see four generations of his family working on the railway before he retired would be fulfilled. He had now been employed by the company for nearly sixty-three years. At seventy-eight he looked much younger than his age; his eyes were still clear and his walk was steady; but his hair was quite white. For some years past he had naturally worked only in the office and sometimes in the workshop, because of course he was slower in his movements, and he realised that he could not respond quickly in an emergency. But he still controlled the day-to-day working of the railway, and also superintended the workshops ; although this did not keep him very busy any longer.

Rhodri was now fifty-six, and growing grey too. Now that only one locomotive was needed every day, he did most of the driving, and his son Hugh went with him as fireman, and drove when his father was off duty for one reason or another or when a second engine was needed in the summer. The only interloper on the Gwernal Valley locomotive staff, otherwise such a strict family monopoly, was a pleasant but rather dull young man who was a spare fireman, and who did odd jobs around the works during the off-season. Until the end of the 1938 season there had been another such young man, who made a second spare fireman for busy days ; but he had gone to seek his fortune abroad, and so there was a vacancy for the coming summer.

Since Hugh's son Gwilym had just turned fourteen and would be leaving school in June, Owen regarded the problem as solved. The job could be kept in the family. When Rhodri pointed out that Gwilym was rather young, Owen disagreed. 'He's a wiry lad, and from the number of times he's been on the engine with you already I've no doubt he could do the job tomorrow,' he said. 'And in any case, he's only a few months younger than I was when I started, and you too, for that matter.' That settled it. And really Owen was by no means the only person who wanted to see son, father, grandfather and great-grandfather working together ; it was a possibility which had been talked about in the village for years, and everybody was pleased to see it happen. There was yet another family celebration, which would have put the one twenty years before to shame ; and the next morning a photograph of the four of them posing in front of *Jennie*, with a long article giving various different, but for the most part recognisable, versions of the family's history appeared in several newspapers. The railway company had a lot of free

159

publicity out of it all, so it had nothing to worry about either.

So for several months during that summer things went very well indeed on the railway; the tourist trade was brisk, the line was busy, and there were no breakdowns or misadventures at all. The sun shone, and the trains went up and down the winding slopes from the coast through the woods and rocks and pastures and heather as regularly as ever. And if Owen sometimes felt, as he sat back and watched it all, a foreboding that it would not last, he had not far to look to find a reason. It's plain to see what the trouble will be, with all this talk of another war, he would say to himself. Still, we lived through the last one here, although not without hurt and loss, and I doubt whether it will be very different this time. And it will doubtless be all over by the time the boy is old enough to fight.

But when disaster first struck at the village, it was nothing that could by any feat of mental gymnastics be blamed on Hitler. The bank, at the end of June, announced that the attempt to make the quarries pay their way again had failed, and there was no prospect of its ever succeeding. The quarrymen were all given a week's notice, and then the quarries closed down; the blow was so sudden and breath-taking that nobody had the spirit to protest. By the middle of July the last loads of slate had been carried away, one or two unsafe working faces had been dynamited, and then a final silence descended on the mountain. One by one the houses began to empty in the village, as the men left to find work in the booming munitions factories. They had seen the columns of smoke and dust of the demolitions from their windows, and it looked to be a final signature of doom. No protest marches would save them now.

Owen knew then that his presentiments had not warned

him of disaster from afar, but at home. For he had learnt that when the quarries had nearly closed in 1936 the directors had discussed whether or not to abandon the railway, and that if the matter had been put to the vote it would have been a very close thing indeed. For while the line would still have been busy enough for a few weeks with the tourists in the summer, it would not have been worth while running at all in the winter, and so more than doubtful whether it could have paid its way.

There had been two factions on the Board; some had said, ' Let's not take the risk, but shut down before we lose all the money we still have, and then with what we get from the scrap merchants we will have something to give the shareholders before we wind up the company.' The others had said, ' No, let's keep the line going as long as we can, and give it a chance—who knows, something might turn up.' But, with the shadow of war looming closer every day, it was plain that nobody would argue in favour of encouraging tourists. There was too much else to worry about. So now Owen realised that the chances that the trains would run after that summer were not so good. ' Well—it's lasted out my time,' was all he could say; but that was a hollow, mocking kind of consolation, and he could get no comfort from it.

But just then it was the busy season once again, and nobody had enough time to think about the future. The heavy trains were fighting up into the newly deserted quarry yard; lemonade bottles were being flung down among the rocks again, defying the polite little notices in the coaches requesting people not to kill platelayers with such objects; and ice-cream papers fluttered like flocks of birds in the mountain wind. Nobody at Port Elwyn one sultry after-noon in the middle of August would have thought that the railway lay under the shadow of extinction. The same crowds surged off the connecting main-line train from along the coast, and thronged the Gwernal Valley platform. For several days past it had been necessary to run an extra train to handle all the people who came ; since the practice of running two engines coupled together at the head of a long train had been stopped recently, as the condition of the viaduct above Hafod Eithaf was giving a little mild anxiety to the company, as it had done to Mr Sullivan more than sixty years before. So now on busy days a second train left Port Elwyn about an hour after the first, and passed it at Abergwernal as it was on its way down again.

That day the first train of the afternoon, six coaches hauled by *Jennie*, left Port Elwyn with Hugh Roberts driving and Gwilym firing. Rhodri and the spare fireman were working the second with *Lady Margaret*.

Gwilym, like Owen before him at the same age, was extremely proud of being a real fireman now, wearing a glossy cap and getting an undeniable, although perhaps rather slim, pay packet at the end of each week. It was not as if the job was new to him ; he could scarcely remember when his father had first taken him for a ride on one of the engines, and while he was still at school he had made quite a number of trips as fireman, unofficially ; and he had long learnt much of all there was to know about it. He had even driven the engines about the yard once or twice. But still, there was certainly a difference between being a schoolboy begging lifts, and being a fully fledged railwayman in his own right. And it was very pleasant to be able to wave down from the cab at friends with whom a few weeks before he had been struggling through the mysteries of algebra and the Tudors and Stuarts, and to say to himself, I'm doing a man's job now, but in a few more weeks you'll be back at that same old grind again.

The sun had been shining when they left the coast, but

great banks of cloud wreathed the mountains, and before long they were in shadow. 'I hope it doesn't start raining,' said Gwilym. 'She'll slip like the devil with this load on a wet rail.'

'So do I,' said his father. 'She's not so steady on her feet as she was ; she needs an overhaul. And of course the more she slips the worse she gets, shaking herself to pieces.'

But the rain held off for a while, and they made the climb up to Garthowen without trouble. When they came over the top of the hill, though, they saw the clouds were low in the valley, and the village and the lake were mantled in soft, drifting curtains of rain.

'Well, we'll be for it on the big climb,' said Hugh. 'I think I'd better nip into the shed while you're taking water and get a bucketful of sand. We may need it.'

Abergwernal was looking at its worst when they drew into the station ; damp and drab and dead. The slate slabs on the platform edges were wet and slippery, and the puddles of water on them reflected the dark sky and the column of black smoke and white steam blowing from *Jennie* across the line and towards the lake. The people on the train shivered in their summer clothes and wondered why on earth they had come.

Hugh was some minutes fetching the sand, and Gwilym had swung back the water column, climbed back into the dry cab, and was waiting before he reappeared, running along the opposite platform with the bucket. Suddenly, as he made to jump down on to the track his boots slipped on the treacherous surface, and he tottered and fell, awkwardly, with the heavy bucket on top and his leg twisted under him. There was a thud and a clatter, and when he started to get up again he suddenly fell back and groaned. Gwilym ran to help him.

'I can't get up,' he said, and his face was white and his voice strained. 'Something's wrong with my leg.' Gwilym could see that. He wondered what to do for a moment, but suddenly noticed that one of the passengers was kneeling beside him, and he seemed to know how to handle the situation.

'Have you got a first-aid kit anywhere?' the man said. 'Go and find one, and get some help. I'm a doctor.'

Gwilym ran across to the station building, where some first-aid equipment was kept. He nearly bumped into Owen, who was coming out to see the reason for the delay. Gwilym told him in a few words.

'Right—bring the outfit over,' Owen said. 'I'll go and see myself what's happening.'

By the time he reached the engine a small crowd had gathered round. He pushed his way through, and carefully bent down to ask the doctor what the matter was.

'Broken leg, I'm afraid,' said the doctor in a low tone. 'He'll have to be sent to hospital. Is there any place in the village?'

'There's a district nurse living just down the road—he'd best go there first of all,' said Owen. Then, with the help of the booking-clerk, who had also appeared, he arranged things. A stretcher was produced, and in five or ten minutes Hugh had been made comfortable and carried off, with the doctor in attendance. So that sudden emergency had been dealt with promptly. But there was another problem now : there was nobody available to drive the train ; the passengers were beginning to grow restive, and *Jennie* was blowing off steam furiously.

Gwilym and the guard were standing beside her, and Owen beckoned to them.

'It looks as if I shall have to take her up myself,' he said. 'I'll just go and put a coat on, and we'll be off in five minutes. Can you get the people back aboard? We're late enough already.'

The guard did this, and Gwilym refilled *Jennie*'s boiler

and attended to the fire, which had burnt low during the delay. Owen gave instructions for a message to be given to the track gang, to say that from tomorrow one of them would have to consider himself transferred to the footplate staff, and then slowly climbed up into the cab.

'We've not worked together before, have we?' he asked Gwilym. 'Well, I don't suppose we will again, either.'

And with that they started. The rain was still pouring down, and the rails were slippery. Gwilym wondered how they would manage with the palsied hand of an old man on the regulator, but he need not have worried. Owen and *Jennie* had grown old together, and the one had no tricks that the other had not long mastered; they forged on up the hill without faltering.

'I didn't think we would get up as well as that,' Gwilym admitted when they stopped in the quarry yard. 'Not on a day like this.'

'Nor with an old dodderer of nearly eighty at the throttle, either, I expect,' said Owen, with his old wry smile.

'I didn't mean that,' said Gwilym, blushing, but Owen chuckled and said, 'Of course you did, lad, and I don't blame you. I haven't driven this old girl on such a day as this for a very long while, and I hardly thought we'd get here either. But falling apart though we may both be, she's still not so bad as she was before she was rebuilt —while she still had Pearson's gear on her. But nobody remembers her like that now,' he added with a sigh.

Gwilym smiled a little nervously, and set about un-coupling the engine and running it round the train for the return journey. He was always a little uncomfortable with his great-grandfather; a strange old man, he thought, always saying something unexpected which might be meant seriously, or might not. He knew, of course, that

Owen had worked on the line when it first opened, when he was hardly older than he was now himself; but it seemed impossible to imagine the upright, white-haired old man as a boy who found the job as new and interesting, even exciting, as he was finding it now.

It was wet and miserable on the mountain, and the passengers were ready and waiting for the return journey. But even at such a wild and now deserted place as this the iron hand of *Bradshaw* ruled sternly, and it could not be imagined that a train should be allowed to leave before the advertised time simply because everybody wanted it to. So for ten minutes they all stood there in silence before the guard pocketed his watch, waved his flag, and with a hiss of steam and a rumble the train rolled off down the hill back to civilisation again.

'We'll ask when we get to the station how your father is getting on,' said Owen.

The doctor was waiting when they arrived, and came up and told them that there was nothing to worry about; an ambulance had already taken Hugh off to the hospital.

'Thank you for telling us—that's a relief,' said Owen, and Gwilym agreed.

'Well, it is to me, too,' said the doctor. 'I've got a connection to catch when we get down to the coast—I have to be in London tomorrow morning.'

'Oh, you'll be all right now,' said Owen. 'We're back on time again.'

Nobody ever found out exactly what happened next, or why. It might have been because Owen was confused, and in his relief on hearing about Hugh forgot what he was doing; but then nobody had ever described him as a muddled old man. It may have been in some measure the guard's fault, who gave the right-away, or even Gwilym's, who should have remembered and realised. Anyhow, for whatever reason, the whole responsibility rested on Owen, and he must carry the blame. For what he and everybody else had forgotten, because of all the disturbance, and did not remember even as the train started and pulled out of the station and up the bank towards Garthowen, was that the other train was running that afternoon, and that it was still on the single line. There were dozens of things that should have reminded someone of this, even if Owen had not made the easy but unforgiveable mistake of leaving without carrying the staff for the section; but nobody was reminded. The only person who realised what had happened was the booking-clerk, who came rushing out on to the platform as soon as he heard *Jennie* start, and ran after the train and shouted as hard as he could; but they did not hear him. And perhaps he had the worst few minutes of all, waiting impotently until the collision sent the echoes rolling for a moment up and down the valley. Then there was utter silence.

## *EPILOGUE*

ABERGWERNAL after four years of war was even more obviously a place which had seen better days. Many of the houses were empty, and their broken windows gazed blindly on to the quiet streets. Some others had been taken over by the army, and were used from time to time while troops were training on the mountains. Perhaps these were now the ugliest of all, as their tiny gardens had been concreted over and hideous brick and tin huts built round about. Only a few were still occupied by the families which had lived in them for years, and were now eking out a living working on the land or for the Forestry Commission. All the houses lacked paint, but these ones were still well kept, and the brass on their doors gleamed brightly, as if defying not only Hitler but also the forces which had laid waste the rest of the village.

Gwilym was in the army now, and this was his final leave before being sent overseas ; so on his last day he was making a pilgrimage to some of the places he had known as a boy, and which he knew he might never see again. He had already climbed the mountain which towered above his home ; grey-green and rock-strewn and unchanged, it seemed to watch the decay of the works of men round its feet with the same lack of interest it had shown when those same men had attacked it and defiled its slopes with quarry scars, and unsightly fans of waste tips. Mere scratches, though, and as mountains reckon time in a little while they would be covered and concealed again by green and living things.

Gwilym turned towards the old station, and followed the path, now overgrown and half blocked, which had been trodden out by his fathers before him. The door to the offices in the station building stood open, creaking in the wind. Inside was a shambles. Plaster had fallen off the walls, and there was a hole in one corner of the roof. The windows were all broken, and in one place the floor had given way and sagged loosely. Everywhere were strewn piles of rotting papers, covered in fading ink with laboriously written details of wagon loadings, freight charges, bills, wage lists, monthly accounts, ticket stocks, and indents ; the meticulously checked, carefully stored waste products of more than sixty years of running trains, now scattered and trampled underfoot. Over on the other side of the yard stood the old workshops and engine and carriage sheds ; their stone walls stood firm and solid enough to last another thousand years ; but they were already relics as useless as Stonehenge. The heavy wooden doors had been pulled down, and lay broken on one side ; the roof had partly collapsed, and what remained no longer kept out the rain, but merely concentrated it in a few places so that it wore gullies in the hard-packed earth floor, for some old man's hens to scratch in.

Gwilym passed these ruins and turned along the course of the railway towards the north. The rails had been lifted for only three years, and it was still possible to see exactly where they had been. Each of them had left a faint, dark impression on the ground, and here and there lay some scrap of forgotten metal still—a spike or bolt or fishplate. In one place, where the engines used to stand for hours between trains, the ground was still paved with a black tarry compound of oil and coaldust, and no grass grew. The few sleepers which had been left behind by the demolition gang had long ago been taken by the soldiers for fuel ; but in spite of the rapid growth of grass and brambles, and the conversion of the cuttings into muddy trenches by the blocked drains, the indentations in the ground where they had been would remain for years to come.

Gwilym walked where the main line had been, not bothering to notice as the tracks of the various sidings converged and finally joined him at the head of the yard. He knew each one of them better than he knew the lines on his hands : and if he shut his eyes he could see them as they had been. As he walked on, the roadbed began to climb. He passed between rank hedges, which were in places almost touching across the way, and through a little wood where he remembered the train once having to stop because a tree had been blown down across the line. Then, they had attacked it with fury, and in twenty minutes the line had been cleared ; now, two trees had lain there for months without anybody lifting a finger. Gwilym scrambled under the last one and continued for another quarter of a mile. When the track emerged from the wood, he turned round to the left and looked back on the village, now below him and more than a mile away, and the long, grey lake beyond it ; and farther and higher up, the farthest ends of the quarry waste tips could just be seen round the shoulder of the mountain. Half a mile farther on, he knew, the line ran over the crest of the ridge, and just past the little stone station at Garthowen he would be able to see the sea glinting in the distance ; but he had come as far as he wanted to. He was standing where the line curved sharply round a rocky bluff, with a drop of some fifteen feet on the other side, and he had just turned and was about to go back when he heard voices and stopped. The last thing he wanted was to meet any tourists, who would be sure to stop him and ask questions ; and these voices seemed to be English. He turned again, and ran on a few yards to a place where the ground came down to track level and there was a gate through the hedge. He vaulted over it, and ran back on the other side of the hedge to where the visitors were standing, treading softly lest they should hear him.

He had been right ; there were three of them. A large, cheerful man of about forty, and his wife, and a boy of about nine. Strange how holidaymakers got about, even in wartime.

' Yes, this is the place,' the man was saying. ' It must have happened just about where I'm standing now—not more than a few yards either way, anyhow.'

' Gosh ! ' said the boy. ' I see now why the driver didn't stop, Dad—he couldn't have seen the other train coming until it was too late, because of the curve, could he ? '

' And what a nasty drop on that side,' said the woman.

' No, it wasn't that,' said the man. ' The train I was in was going this way—downhill, you see—and the other one was going uphill. But I definitely remember that our brakes went on very hard at least ten seconds before the crash, so we must have seen them.'

'How fast were you going?' asked the boy.

'Oh, about twenty miles an hour, I suppose. It was about as fast as the thing could go. But we had slowed down a little when we hit.'

'I suppose your driver must have seen the smoke of the other engine, then, over the top of the hedge. But what happened when they hit?'

'Well, our engine went over the edge of the bank about here, and landed on its nose, almost, in the field. I suppose they made these marks pulling it back again. One of the coaches followed it, and another had its side torn off and went half-way down the bank—the others, including the one I was in, were just lifted off the track and knocked a bit sideways. The other engine had its cab bashed in, and was thrown against the side of the cutting—look, you can still see the marks on the rock. This must be the right place. The rest of the train wasn't too badly hit—the first coach had its end knocked in and went over the side, but at any rate none of the passengers was hurt.'

'Was anybody killed?' The boy asked the inevitable question.

'Only one man,' replied his father. 'The old man who was driving the other train, the one coming up the hill.'

'Gosh, it must have been a bad accident, Dad.'

'Yes, it was—quite bad enough for me. Still, it's not everybody who's been in a railway smash, even on a tin-pot line like this one. Gives you something to talk about. But it beats me how it ever stayed on the rails.' He paused for a moment, chuckling at his little joke, and gazing round appreciatively. Then he said, 'Come on, let's get back to the car. We've a long way to go today yet.'

'What a morbid place to think of getting out to see,' said the woman as they moved away. 'I suppose children are always bloodthirsty, but I've seen quite enough for today.'

172

Gwilym, who had been standing silently behind the hedge listening to all this, sat down and buried his face in his hands. He was very glad he had avoided those people, now he had heard their talk. For that day was one that he would never forget. He still remembered, and it kept coming back to him when he couldn't sleep at night. Owen's shout as he suddenly saw the black smoke that *Lady Margaret* was making as she coasted down the grade, and the vicious thud and grind of the brakes. He remembered seeing *Lady Margaret* appear round the curve, still running hard, and how terrifyingly quickly she had grown bigger, and the tiny flying figures as her driver and fireman jumped out. He jumped too, and turned over and over as he fell, but Owen had left it too late. What happened next was a confused memory of bright colours and slow motion, and no certainty of what came next. He seemed to fall for ages. The rending, ringing, crumpling crash as the engines hit, which seemed to go on for hours. He was on his back in the hedge, trapped somehow under the first coach, which must have followed him through the air. And there was another noise, too, apart from the roaring of escaping steam ; somebody screaming ; it might almost have been himself, but he couldn't remember. And then, somehow, slowly, the black pit, until who knows how much later he woke up and found himself in hospital.

Then things became clear again, and he remembered the hospital very distinctly until the day they let him out and he went home again, his legs in plaster. And then there was the awful business of going to the enquiry, and giving evidence. When the report came out, and laid the whole blame for the collision on Owen, as of course it was bound to, he had wondered how any member of the family could ever hold up his head in the village again ; but he had been heartened by the understanding of the valley folk, who at any rate, unlike the Inspector, had the memory of Owen's sixty years of service on the railway to set against the under-standable lapse of an old man's memory. The accident was a bad business, indeed ; but it was just one of those things which might have happened to anybody. And had not the manner of Owen's death done something to lessen the fault ? For he had stayed on his engine to the last, hoping that he might still avert the collision ; and he had paid for this with his life. And so after a while Gwilym began to feel that just as his family had shared in the glory of the railway, so their part in its downfall had not been entirely shameful.

For it was the accident which finally decided the fate of the line, even though the wreckage was cleared in the next few days, and trains ran again for a little while. For the company had very little money now, and there seemed no hope of making any without the quarries' working ; then there was the war ; and finally the expense of repairing the two locomotives and the coaches to consider. So the last train ran, quietly and with no celebration (it was hardly the time for it) when the war was a few weeks old. And then the scrap men came and tore the line apart.

Men with rending acetylene torches sliced up *Jennie* and *Lady Margaret* in the yard, and drops of their melted metal could still be found if you poked about in the turf. The coaches had been burned, and the metal parts raked from the ashes ; and the track had been lifted by a gang which started work in the quarry yard and in a few weeks had carted all the rail down to Port Elwyn, where it was stacked in several enormous piles. ' This is an urgent job,' they had said. ' We need this scrap metal for the war effort.'

And so the demands of total war had been used to silence the voices of those few who had thought that when the shadow had passed, a way might yet be found to have the trains running up the valley once again, like other things that men were hoping to see once more. But now, as a final irony, the rails were still piled there ; and *Lady Gwyneth* and

174

*Rhodri Mawr*, first Prince of Wales, still stood rusty and battered and derelict in the open air ; all forgotten.

But now, when he heard those trippers talking of that evil afternoon, something inside Gwilym seemed to give way. Everything else could be borne ; but not the ignorant laughter of ghouls who came to snigger and make fun. Till that moment he had always planned to return to Abergwernal after the war, to try and pick up some of the threads of the life he had known as a boy. But now the past vanished and his mind seemed to clear. It was no use. The railway was dead, and that chapter over and done with. It didn't matter if it did mean leaving his relations who still lived there, his father and grandfather, and his great-grandmother Elizabeth, who still lived on, quiet and untouched by all change, in a room in which everything seemed to hold some memory of Owen and his work.

' No, it's no good at all,' he said out loud, addressing an old sheep who just stared back at him, chewing stoically. ' I'll just have to get out and start again somewhere else. Haunted castles are all very well, but you can't live in them.'

He crossed the old railway and took the path home across the fields, not looking back at all.

www.ingramcontent.com/pod-product-compliance
Lightning Source LLC
Chambersburg PA
CBHW030505260626
47157CB00005B/1666